A NOVEL BY

LUMPING

RON ABRAYTIS

𝒯RUBS?

The Writers Block Publishing Company, North Augusta, South Carolina

A WRITERS BLOCK PUBLISHING COMPANY
FIRST EDITION COPYRIGHT ©1995 BY RON ABRAYTIS

Published in the United States of America by
The Writers Block Publishing Company
P.O. Box 6337, North Augusta, SC 29841

Book and cover design by Company B Graphics
Cover Photo ©1994 by David Grinnell

Books published by The Writers Block Publishing Company are
available at special quantity discounts for bulk purchases for sales
promotions, premiums, fund raising or educational use.

For details write:
The Writers Block Publishing Company
P.O. Box 6337, N. Augusta, SC 29841

Abraytis, Ron, 1953-
    Are you clumping trubs? : a novel/Ron Abraytis.
        p.   cm.
    ISBN 1-881555-14-3 (paperback): $10.95
    I. Title.
    PS3551.B74A89 1995
    813' .54—dc20   94-37561
                                                          CIP

To Kate

Once a day, every day, all day long

QUICK GUIDE TO THE CHARACTERS

Jerry Applegate:	*Migraine consultant, care-giver for people with AIDS, and neophyte to the gay world*
Chardonnay:	*Flamboyant migraine client of Applegate*
Charles:	*More serious migraine client*
Dutchman:	*AIDS client of Applegate*
Calvin:	*Dutchman's sometimes-lover, sometimes-enemy*
Pinkerton:	*Friend to Calvin, possible psycho, possible murderer*
Ogden:	*Friend to Dutchman, disgusted with the bar scene*
Elyssia:	*Applegate's friend, 75 years old, likes to play pinochle*
Rosencrantz and Guildenstern:	*Frisky gay lovers you don't ever want to see in your bathroom at night*
Dr. Bellman:	*Applegate's analyst*
Raymond:	*Affectionate Vietnam vet from Michigan who Applegate meets in a bar*
Matthew Bumpers:	*Bookstore owner, intrigued by Applegate's smile*
Winston and Carlyle:	*Friends of Matthew who enjoy hanging around his bookstore and discussing politics*
Throckmorton and Paris:	*Drinking buddies of Matthew, screaming queens*
Kevin and Alex:	*Lovers who fight a great deal*
Jacques Hardoné:	*Star of gay video porn*

$\mathcal{O}$NE

"Dutchman! Dutchman! A man approached me in a gay bar!"

"Hi, Applegate, come on in."

Applegate stood in the doorway and said, "I'm serious! A man talked to me in a gay bar! What should I have done?"

Dutchman took his arm and led him into the foyer. "First give me your coat. Is this my birthday gift?"

Applegate handed him the turquoise-wrapped box. "Yeah. Happy birthday." He kissed Dutchman on the cheek, then followed him into the living room, whispering excitedly, "So I was standing there…"

Dutchman said, "I don't think you know anyone except Calvin and Ogden. Let me introduce you. Everybody, this is my social worker, Jerry Applegate."

"I'm not a social worker!"

"Applegate, this is…" and Dutchman went around the room, pointing and naming names.

Applegate was much too excited to listen. At the first opportunity he pulled Dutchman into the kitchen and said, "A man spoke to me! In a gay bar! He asked what kind of beer I was drinking. Is that a come-on?"

Dutchman smiled and poured himself a white wine and soda. "Probably. Where were you?"

"The Blue Gardenia."

"Definitely a come-on. That's a meat rack. What were you doing there?"

"I don't know. I just happened to walk in. It was real close."

"It's nowhere near your apartment!"

"No, but it's right down the block from my analyst."

"How convenient!"

Applegate said, "This was my second time there. I like to stand and look. I enjoy watching... you know, men touching each other."

"You mean the porno videos?"

"No. Well, yes. I mean, I like them too. But I was talking about men dancing together, hugging each other. I like to watch. You know, I figure, in a place like that, I'll be safe."

Dutchman sipped his wine spritzer. "Safe? Safe from what?"

"Well, not safe exactly. But I mean, no one's going to approach me."

"Don't you want to be approached?"

"Of course I do!"

"But you go to a bar like the Blue Gardenia because you figure it won't happen there."

Applegate shrugged. "I like it. But I know that no one's going to plow their way through the crowd of gorgeous young men in tight jeans and leather jackets to get to me. I figure I can go there and watch undisturbed."

"Even though a man did plow his way to you."

Applegate began pacing, his face aglow. "It was so weird! I was standing there alone, drinking my beer, watching the porno videos–"

"We're back to them!"

"Yeah. I like them. A lot! My analyst thinks it's good for me. You know, for me to see what men can do sexually."

"Why don't you just get yourself a man to practice with, honey?"

"That's a little advanced for me at this point."

Dutchman smiled. "A shrink who prescribes pornography and lives down the block from a meat-rack tavern. Maybe I should start going to this guy. Sounds like my kind of therapy."

"But what does it mean? My second time in this bar, and a man talks to me. What did he want?"

"Maybe he liked your body."

In exasperation Applegate said, "Dutchman! I'm serious! What does it mean?"

"Sometimes you're too much."

"Come on! I'm twenty-nine, I'm inexperienced–"

Dutchman put his hand on his hip and asked, "Just how did he know you' so inexperienced?"

"I think it's tattooed on my forehead."

"Let me check." He took Applegate's head in his hands and examined his face.

He sighed and said very seriously, "You're right, it is there for anyone to read."

"So what did he want?"

"What did you say to him?"

"I told him it was Weiss beer."

"And?"

"He asked if it doesn't usually come with a slice of lemon."

"What did you say?"

"It usually does, but I asked the bartender not to put it in."

Dutchman nodded sagely. "Sounds like you really swept him off his feet with lines like that. Then what?"

"He walked away."

Calvin came in with an empty glass. "What's going on in here? Party's in the living room."

"Applegate done met him a man tonight!"

"Good, then maybe you'll stop chasing after my Dutchman. Gimme kiss, sweetie!"

As the liver-lips approached, Dutchman gave him a shove and said, "Get you' brandy and leave Applegate and me to our girl-talk."

Calvin laughed–very unconvincingly–and walked out with a vengeful glare aimed at Applegate.

Dutchman said, "He don't like you yet."

"Does he like anyone?"

"Dutchman! Baby!" Mike walked in and gave Dutchman a hug, which Dutchman warmly returned.

There began a trickle of guests coming in for drinks or snacks. Dutchman whispered, "Three guesses who sent them all in here."

The conversation swirled and danced around the room. Every few minutes Applegate's excited voice could be heard above the noise, "So getting back to this man in the bar…"

Lance, a beautiful black man Applegate had just met for the first time tonight, said, "Yes, I believe I did hear you bellowing something about him before–"

Ogden broke in, "What bar?"

"The Blue Gardenia."

"That's a pick-up bar!"

Applegate said wistfully, "For some people, maybe…"

Ogden was incensed. "It's a pick-up bar I'm telling you! He was probably giving you a line! I don't go to bars anymore; all they want is sex."

"Not from me."

"It was a line. A come-on. What did he say?"

"He asked me what kind of beer I was drinking."

Ogden sounded disgusted. "How transparent! He really wanted a one-night stand!"

Now Applegate was interested. "No kidding? Are you sure? 'Cause he might still be there."

Ogden was oblivious. "Know what I would have said?"

Applegate was breathless. "What?! Tell me, maybe if I hurry—"

"I would have said, 'Why? You wanna buy me one?' That would have shut him up!"

"No, I didn't want—"

"Of course not, you didn't want to go home with some cheap tramp from a sleazy—"

"Not go home? Well, a motel…"

"That's all they want! I've heard it all, all the lines!"

Applegate looked at Ogden closely. If a plain-looking, short, hawk-nosed curmudgeon like Ogden was approached all the time…

Lance said, "Ogden, darling, Applegate liked the man."

Ogden was flabbergasted. "What?"

"The man in the bar. He wanted to talk to him."

Ogden looked at Applegate. "Really?"

"Well, that's the general idea."

"Haven't you had enough of that shallow, sleazy, sex-oriented—"

"'Enough' is a relative term."

Lance eased himself in front of Ogden and smiled at Applegate. "So you liked him?"

"Yes."

Lance took center stage. Ogden fixed a brandy and 7-Up and muttered to himself, "Why? You wanna buy me one, big mouth?" He turned angrily to Calvin and said, "That would have shut him up!"

Calvin, eyeing Dutchman standing a little too close to Philip, said just as angrily as Ogden, "Yeah! Lousy horny bastards!"

More guests trickled in, ostensibly for wine or beer, but lingered long after their glasses were full.

Lance was saying, "You see a man you like, you make your move before someone else grabs him. Now, I'll be the guy. What was his name?"

Applegate was embarrassed to admit, "I don't know."

Lance rolled his eyes. "Honey, that's the first thing you find out. Rule number one: a person's own name is the most important word in the language to him. You find it out and use it all you can. It's especially effective when accompanied by a touch on the elbow. Rule number two is plenty of eye contact."

"Eye contact is important?"

"Are you kidding? Eye contact is everything!"

Applegate got very excited. "We made eye contact!"

A newcomer asked, "Who did?"

Applegate turned excitedly to the newcomer and said, "Me and dreamboat! In the bar! After he walked away, I looked over to him a couple times, and he was looking at me!"

Lance said, "Excellent! Then what?"

Applegate's excitement visibly deflated. "Then what? You mean I should have done something?"

Lance sighed and rubbed his forehead. "You just looked at him?"

"No."

"Well?"

"I… uh, I turned away."

"You turned away?"

The newcomer asked, "Why did you turn away? Was he a pervert?"

Ogden said, "It was a line!"

Lance rolled his eyes, "Will you stop with the fucking lines?"

"But that's my point! It was a fuck-line!"

Lance asked Applegate, "Why did you turn away?"

"I got scared."

"You mean you looked up, he was looking at you…"

"And I just fluttered my hands and turned back to the TV."

"This may take longer than I thought. Sit down. Good. You're drinking your beer, I'm standing over here–" he walked across to Dutchman and Philip "–with my buddies. Right? I see you. I think, 'Hmmmm, there's an interesting man. Could be a college professor. Maybe a freelance artist.' I tell my friends–" he indicated Dutchman and Philip, both of whom were now fully involved in the unfolding drama "–that I'm going over to check you out. So I walk across the room–" he did so "–and nod at you."

Applegate was sitting stiffly on his stool, observing Lance with a serious, intent look on his face. Lance walked up to him, looked down longingly into his eyes a moment, and nodded. He asked in a deep, manly growl, "What kind of beer you drinking?"

The nod, the voice–the look in Lance's eyes!–were a little too potent. Applegate tried to keep in mind that it was only an exercise, but as he returned the nod, he got lost in Lance's smile. "Uhhhhhhhh…"

Lance forged ahead. With a sultry, slithering, narcotic drawl, he asked, "What's your name, good looking?"

Applegate stared open-mouthed, glaze-eyed. Finally he said, "Weiss."

"What?!"

"No, I mean Applegate. What? My name? Or my beer? What?"

Lance laughed. "You got to be cool. I'll try again. This time–" Lance, standing very close to Applegate, subtly reached out and held his hand while he talked "–mellow out a little. When I come over–" Applegate listened intently, wondering what that thing was that was wrapped around his fingers "–just give me a nod, look me up and down." Applegate's eyes automatically glanced Lance up and down, and he noticed Lance's hand holding his. He gave a start but quickly recovered and hoped Lance hadn't noticed. Lance did not let go. "Just let it happen, okay?"

Applegate tried to decipher the meaning of the hand-holding. Lance was so laid-back he seemed unaware he was doing it.

Lance crossed the room and again stood with Dutchman and Philip. He pretended to be checking Applegate out. He strolled over and put his hand on the back of Applegate's neck. Applegate felt all his vertebrae melt. Lance said, "I hope I'm not being too forward, but I saw your sweet self sitting alone and I thought, 'What a waste of sin!'"

Lance's obscene tone bypassed Applegate's ears and penetrated directly to his groin. Lance's eyes–sparkling, playful, imploring–harpooned him.

When Applegate didn't respond (except to moan), Lance asked, "What' you drinking, baby?"

"Whatever you want me to drink."

"No, what's that in your hand?"

"Apple juice. I mean, beer."

Lance tried again. "What kind of beer, you sweet, sexy thaang?"

"Uhhhhhh…"

Yvonne broke in, "That's not how men flirt! Not wit' women!"

Lance, along with the rest of the room, turned to look at her. Yvonne continued, "I'll show you. You be the woman, I'll be the man." She turned around, her back to everyone, and pretended to turn up her nonexistent collar. Then she faced Lance, shaking her arms out from the elbows and shuffling towards him with an arrogant strut. Suddenly she cupped her hand along her inner thigh, midway between her groin and knee, and began shouting, "I got the big 12-inch! Yeah baby! Right here! I got it! 12 big ones!"

Lance said, "Get real! Besides, Applegate–"

Yvonne spun on Applegate and yelled right into his face, "Twelve inches! Right here! Come on honey!"

Philip walked over and said, "Okay, I'll be the man in the bar. Mike! You be Applegate."

Mike sat demurely and crossed his legs. He asked, "Am I a man or a woman?"

"You're Applegate here."

"I repeat–"

"Bitch! Dutchman, you be Applegate." Dutchman immediately gaped at Lance. Philip said, "That's right. Just like Applegate."

Calvin muttered, "Lousy horny goats!" Ogden commiserated with him.

Philip said, "Here we go. Now, I walk over to Dutchman and I play it cool. I stand next to him, pretend I'm watching the videos, then I subtly turn my head." He looked at Dutchman. "I ask, 'how you doing tonight, buddy?'"

Dutchman responded, "I'm okay. How're you?"

"Lot of dogs here. Don't you hate seeing the same tired old queens night after night?" Everyone in the room automatically glanced over at Calvin, then quickly turned away.

Philip said to Applegate, "What I find effective at this point is to just reach out and…" He placed his hand on Dutchman's crotch.

Dutchman responded by writhing erotically and moaning, "Yeah, baby, let's go, right here!"

Philip turned to Applegate, "See? It works every time."

Calvin said, "Okay, demonstration's over. You can take your hand away now."

Philip looked at him innocently. "What?"

"Your hand. It's still on my Dutchman's dick."

"Is it?" He looked down. "So it is."

The conversation broke up into several small huddles, all with the same theme.

"This guy sat next to me once and said, 'I'm married. Can I buy you a drink?' It worked on me."

"What line hasn't worked on you?"

"I went home with this stud-muffin who said we were going to practice totally safe sex. I swear to God, we did it in separate rooms. Wasn't bad either. Kind of like phone sex."

"I had this guy come up to me and deliberately step on my feet. When I looked at him, he said, 'Sorry, but I just got off my *yacht* and I don't have my land-legs back yet.'"

Yvonne said, "Now if I'm trying to pick up a woman, I tell her the truth. If I like her hair, I say so. Or if I only want to talk, I go up to her and start, 'You look interesting. Can we talk a while?' Women don't go through all the bullshit you men do."

The cigarette smoke in the kitchen was getting to be a little too much for Dutchman; even when he'd had an immune system, he'd been sensitive to smoke. Now…

He slipped away into the other room. There, on the round table, in the circle of peach-colored light given off by the lamp in the center of the table, was the present Applegate had brought him.

Dutchman sat in the leather easy chair next to the table and picked up the turquoise-wrapped package.

It suddenly seemed quiet, sitting alone in this dimly-lit room, after the laughing and yelling in the kitchen. He could still hear them, of course, but he felt like he was in a little circle of calm, a circle as small and fragile as the circle of light from the lamp. He felt protected and isolated, yet fearful of the gift in his hands. He knew what it would be.

Dutchman unwrapped it. It was a copy of *And the Band Played On* by Randy Shilts. A history of the AIDS epidemic. Applegate and Dutchman had just seen it a few weeks ago, when they were out shopping. Applegate had asked Dutchman if he had read it. Dutchman had said no.

What Dutchman hadn't told Applegate was that he was afraid of such books; he was afraid of all the meetings and discussion groups and those angry young men on T.V. shouting, "Silence Equals Death!"

He opened the cover. On the first blank page was written: "This book can make you crazy. I hope it makes you angry! Your friend, Jerry Applegate."

His reverie was broken by Ogden walking in from the kitchen. He asked Dutchman, "You okay, buddy?"

"I'm fine. I just wanted to open Applegate's gift." He held it up for Ogden to see. "What do you think?"

Ogden ignored the book. "What do I think? I know what I would have done! I would have thrown my beer in the guy's face and told him, 'Here's what I'm drinking!' That would have shut him up!"

TWO

Dr. Bellman sat back, fingers casually interlocked, and asked, "Then what happened?"

The grandfather clock ticked loudly in the quiet room. Applegate's breathing was quick and heavy. His chest rose and sank spasmodically. He swallowed a sob and said, "Well, you know, the party was going on, we all kind of wandered around the apartment… Dutchman put out some food, there was music and dancing in the dining room… and I didn't see that much of Lance. Dutchman kept telling me to ask him to dance, but I was too nervous."

"Did Lance dance with anyone else?"

"No, he just watched the others."

"Then what?"

A tear spilled over Applegate's cheek. His voice trembled, "Well, I decided to leave. So I went to Lance, and I said, 'I have another scene for you. Let's say I meet you at a party, and I want to see you again. How could I tell you that?'"

Dr. Bellman laughed. "How did he respond?"

Applegate reached for a kleenex. "Lance smiled. He said I was doing it just fine. I asked him for his phone number. He gave it to me…"

"And then you got scared?"

Applegate looked at Dr. Bellman with pain and wonder. "Yeah, I got scared. Terrified. How did you know?"

"With your history, it would be amazing if you hadn't been frightened.

What did you say?"

"I got angry..."

"Go on."

"I raised my voice..."

"Yes."

"I said... I said I knew it was all a trick. I said I knew this was just some practical joke he was playing, and that he was taking the joke too far by giving me his number."

"What was his reaction?"

"Oh, Dr. Bellman, he looked so hurt. I was actually yelling at him, actually yelling that he had no right to lead me on like that..."

"It never occurred to you that he liked you." Dr. Bellman made the comment as a statement of fact, not a question.

"I knew it was just a trick... a stupid joke... but when I yelled at him, the look on his face... I don't know. He was so hurt."

"Did you ever call him?"

"I called him the next day, left a message on his machine. He never called back. I don't blame him. I acted like such a psycho. But I swear, I swear I did not know he was being sincere."

"You were frightened. It was too much too soon. Because of your childhood, intimacy and horror are entwined together. Rape is one of the most devastating traumas a human being can experience. When it happens at such a young age, and the rapist is your own father, it goes to the very heart of your capacity to form relationships with other people. It's going to take a while before you accept the fact that a man could find you attractive. Right now the concept is far too threatening."

Applegate seemed calmer. "I go so nuts when I think a guy likes me. I always thought it was gay men keeping me out, that it was them who wouldn't let me in. You know, the *Jerry Applegate Newsletter*."

Dr. Bellman laughed. "The *Jerry Applegate Newsletter?*"

"I had this image that every time I try to come out, all you gay men in Chicago circulate the *Jerry Applegate Newsletter* announcing that I was at it again and to stay away from me. Now I know... it's something inside me, it's me that won't let gay men get close."

"Like with Lance the other night."

"Yeah. I guess he liked me. And I went off, yelling at him."

"We have to take it slow. You went to a gay party. That's a start. You met a gay man you liked. That in itself is an accomplishment."

"I used to always fall for straight men. Now I'm starting to find gay men fascinating."

"That means you're opening up to the idea of a romantic involvement.

While you were falling in love with straight men, you were sabotaging yourself, staying in a safe, if painful, place. Now you're beginning to reach out to possibilities of intimacy."

"Dr. Bellman, when that man in the bar asked me what kind of beer I was drinking–I mean, the whole room changed. Like it lit up. No, it was more like a door opening… just a crack… but it was opened for the first time. It felt like friendship. It was like a glimpse of… of some kind of palace."

"I know how anxious you are. You want to plunge in. But maybe you'll have to go slow, just test the water a little at a time until you can handle it. There's one thing I want to talk about. It's this business of my prescribing pornography."

"I thought you said it was okay."

"The point is, it's not my decision whether it's okay or not okay. I don't prescribe things for you. I don't tell you what to do. If you want to watch pornography, that's fine with me. I see benefits. I see drawbacks. We talk about it. But you make the decision."

"I still view you sometimes as an authority figure."

"We've spoken before of your confusing me with your father."

Applegate felt a shudder of horror. "Yeah, sometimes you look just like him."

"Even though I bear no physical resemblance to him."

"I get so scared when that happens…"

"It's all part of the transference. When you start to trust me, you feel vulnerable and that inspires terror. You see me as a demon who's trying to hurt you. Or you split into one of the other little boys. Or you get away from me by floating out of your body the same way you did that time your father burned you with soldering iron. Just keep reminding yourself that the hallucinations were your tools for keeping your sanity at a time when your world was quite literally insane. They were coping mechanisms that helped you survive."

Applegate rearranged himself on the sofa and said, "You know, sometimes I think maybe I should just go out and hire a hustler. Pay him fifty bucks or whatever and get it over with."

"You could. But first ask yourself, what are the chances of a hustler giving you what you want? Can a hustler give you love? Or just a dick up your ass?"

"I know you're not telling me what to do. But it sure sounds like you're trying to guide me."

"I don't want to see you waste time going down dead-ends. With AIDS, one mistake could be fatal."

Applegate sighed. "The first time I make love with a man, I want it to be real gentle and calm. I don't want him to start screaming and going crazy. That would scare me." He pondered a moment and smiled. "But I think I'll get over that fear real fast!"

"There are dozens of things you and a lover can do with each other.

Pornography can be wonderful. It can teach you things. It can make you feel good about your body. When you have a lover, the two of you can watch it together to get ideas and discuss your feelings. You and your lover can settle in with Jacques Hardoné or Kevin Williams, and it livens up an evening. There's the Pleasure Chest, a whole store full of toys, rubber and leather novelties, dildos, butt-plugs. There's mutual masturbation, or watching each other masturbate. There's dancing and hand-holding and romance."

Applegate felt frightened by Dr. Bellman's words. Finally he said, "I don't know. When I walk into a room full of gay men, I wonder what they will want from me."

"Yes, Applegate, what will they want?"

Applegate thought a long time. Finally he said, "I don't even know what I want from them."

"What do you fantasize about men?"

A long pause. "Being kissed."

"Go on."

"I think that must be the best of all–to be kissed by a man. I think of that more than anything else, more than sex, more than passion–I think of kissing a man."

$\mathscr{T}$HREE

Guildenstern asked, "Hey, Rosencrantz, what's this funny yellow powder?"
"It's called Roach Away."
"What's it for?"
Rosencrantz glanced nonchalantly over his shoulder and answered, "Supposedly, we get it on our legs, drag it back to the nest, and it kills the whole colony."
Guildenstern jumped in the air. "Holy cow! What'll we do?"
Rosencrantz, as always, remained calm. "For heaven's sake! It's been on the market for months! We all developed immunity to it an hour after Applegate brought it into the building." His little cockroach ears pricked up. "Hey, I hear him coming."
Guildenstern quickly scanned left and right and shouted, "Let's run!"
Rosencrantz kept an eye on the bathroom door. "Will you relax! We have plenty of time. Okay! He's about to turn on the light. When he does, start rolling around in the Roach Away."
"Why?"
"Because it will totally jam that little brain of his. Now!" The bathroom lit up. Rosencrantz and Guildenstern frolicked in the yellow powder.
Rosencrantz kept an ocular antenna on Applegate as he said, "Okay, we have a few seconds before he–"
Guildenstern strained forward and yelled, "What? I can't hear you over the screaming."

"I said, we have a few seconds before he goes for the–RUN!!!"

Applegate returned with the can of Raid. Rosencrantz shouted, "This way! Behind the tub."

They escaped just in time, running inside the wall with the scent of Raid at their heels. When they were safe, Rosencrantz rolled on his back laughing. "I like him, I really do. It's fun to see how nuts he goes."

Guildenstern was worriedly licking at his legs. "I don't know. Seems kind of a dangerous way to get your kicks."

Rosencrantz observed him licking off the Roach Away and said, "Not so fast! That yellow sheen makes you real sexy."

Guildenstern stopped in mid-lick. "Yeah?"

Rosencrantz kissed him on the facial exoskeleton. "Don't worry about Applegate. The day that molasses brain can get me–"

"You enjoy tormenting him like that?"

"Sure, but seriously, I like him. I would never hurt him."

"Hurt him?"

Rosencrantz shrugged and said, "You know, crawl in his ear at night and lay eggs."

"Can boys lay eggs?"

"Honey, we're roaches. We can do anything. We are omnipotent and omnipresent."

"I didn't know that."

"Stick with me, you'll learn something."

"So, what do you want to do tonight?"

"I don't know. What do you want to do?"

"I don't know."

"We could go by the tub in 310. There's always action there after midnight."

"The same tired old queens we see at the kitchen sink in 407 every Tuesday."

"Guildenstern, did you ever think of moving? I mean, picking up and leaving altogether? I hear it's a lot nicer three doors west. They say it's dark there from 4:00 p.m. to 10:00 a.m. every day, the pipes leak, crumbs and scraps everywhere, the people never even heard of personal hygiene…"

"Sounds like paradise."

"So what do you want to do tonight?"

"Why don't we just stay in and see if we can watch some other couple mating? Those guys in 213 are into leather."

"Woof!"

$\mathcal{F}$OUR

Applegate had no idea what the chances were that the stranger would be at the Blue Gardenia again. But no power on this earth could keep him from going back next week.

Applegate was there on a Sunday evening, sipping his Weiss beer, standing against the wall, watching the porno videos.

As it happened, two men settled in near him and began speaking. Applegate pretended to ignore them, but he could hear their conversation clearly:

"So then he says he wants ten dollars! Ten dollars! When I was a kid, I cut lawns for a quarter!"

"Can you believe kids these days?"

"Ten dollars! I had a paper route! I got up at five a.m. to walk three miles delivering papers!"

"Right, three miles, sure, uh-huh!"

"Five a.m.! And I saved my pennies until I could buy a bike!"

"Buy a bike. With your own money. Sure, sure."

"And then I walked into the bank with my pennies and I said to Mr. Johnson, 'I'm here to cash in my change so I can buy a bike.' And he said, 'Good boy!'"

"Good boy!"

Applegate listened without turning to look at the two men. Somehow the atmosphere tonight was not sparkling, the talk did not scintillate. As the story of the paper route unfolded, Applegate was astonished to think that gay men could actually be boring.

A short, wiry man at the bar got off his stool and lumbered towards the washroom in the back. As he wavered and sputtered he passed near Applegate, touched Applegate on the chest with one finger and said, "Saw you at the bar," and kept going.

Applegate considered the words... "Saw you at the bar"? Did he mean he once saw Applegate sitting at the bar? Or that the stranger had been at the bar and saw Applegate? Applegate knew intuitively that the man would speak to him again.

Sure enough, a few minutes later, the stranger came and stood by Applegate's shoulder. Applegate concentrated on all that he had learned at Dutchman's party last week. The first rule was get his name.

The stranger stood there a few moments. Applegate turned and faced him. The stranger smiled. Applegate nodded and said, "Hi."

The stranger slurred his words, "How're you doin' t'night?"

Applegate was amused and flattered that a stranger would approach him. "Just fine."

"Everyone calls me Terry."

"Applegate."

"Looking for a little action tonight?"

Applegate interpreted the question in its broadest sense and answered, "Oh, not exactly. That's not really why I come here." He glanced over at Terry. Terry was smiling in a very provocative way. Applegate asked in sudden astonishment, "Are you asking? I mean, asking me?"

Terry shrugged a moment, looking unsure, and then quickly recovered. He threw back his shoulders and proudly announced, "Yeah I'm asking."

Applegate fumbled for words. Terry was somewhat attractive–physically attractive, although the extreme drunkenness and slurred speech detracted from his appeal.

Applegate glowed as he said, "Well, gee, that's real nice... I mean, I don't..."

"And I could give you a discount if you let me sleep over."

Suddenly the glow was gone. Terry was looking defiantly at Applegate.

"A discount?"

"Sure. Usually I charge fifty. If you let me stay over, I'll only charge twenty."

"I see. I take it you're a... a gentleman of the evening?"

"No, I'm a hustler. They call me the king of the hustlers around here."

Applegate felt more sad than foolish. Terry was a pathetic burlesque of a hustler. His body was firm and muscular, but his face deeply lined with alcoholism. His hair was full but ragged. At one time he must have been a handsome man. Now he could be a distinguished older man if he gave even minimal attention to his appearance. But Applegate couldn't imagine anyone paying Terry in his present condition.

Applegate said, "Well, like I said, I'm really not here for that tonight. But can I buy you a beer?"

"Sure."

Applegate noted the bottle in Terry's hand. "Miller?"

Terry hesitated a moment before pointing to Applegate's glass. "I'd rather have one of those."

"You want a Weiss?"

"Well, if you don't mind. I mean, I know it costs more—"

"Don't be silly. I'd be glad to buy you one." Applegate left and returned in a minute with two tall glasses of Weiss beer, each decorated with a slice of lemon.

"So, how long have you been hustling?"

Terry took a long, deep drink of his beer and said, "Oh, couple years now."

"I bet you have a lot of stories you could tell."

"Baby, I could tell you stories would make you cry."

Applegate waited. Terry sipped his beer but said no more. After a minute, Applegate asked, "Well, go ahead. Tell me about your experiences."

"You can't believe the life of a hustler. The people I've met, the places I been…" He took another drink of beer. Again, the stories were not forthcoming. Terry was so drunk that he couldn't keep track of the conversation.

In order to prime the pump, Applegate asked, "What's the biggest tip you've ever gotten?"

Terry proudly announced, "Fifty dollars!" Then he quickly added, "That's just the tip! Fifty dollar tip on top of the fifty dollar charge."

Applegate was abysmally disappointed. And saddened. Fifty dollars seemed a dismally small amount for the highest tip in a career of hustling. He continued trying to get Terry to relate some of his stories, but Terry, drunk and distracted, couldn't concentrate enough to oblige Applegate.

Eventually Terry wandered away.

Applegate decided to stay a while longer. He noticed another man sitting nearby on a barstool, leaning against the wall. He smiled and nodded at Applegate.

Applegate tried to process all that was happening. Last week, the nice man had asked him what kind of beer he was drinking. Probably he was flirting. Tonight, Terry approached him for money. So all friendly faces in a gay bar are not after the same thing. Now a third man was acting friendly. What did he want?

Applegate and the man began chatting about the porno video. The man said, "My name is Andrew."

"Hi, Andrew. Applegate."

"Hi."

Applegate said, "I've been having a strange evening."

"Yeah, I saw you talking with Terry. He's a character."

"You know him?"

"Everyone knows Terry. The grand-dad of the hustlers."

"He said the king of the hustlers."

"Maybe twenty years ago."

Applegate looked confused. "Plus before I was talking to him, I was listening to the most boring conversation you could imagine. These two guys were bitching and moaning about kids today, how spoiled they are now, how hard they had to work when they were kids. I swear, it was like a broken record of every cliche that parents have ever used on their kids. I didn't know–I honestly never thought–that gay men could be so shallow and boring."

Andrew was glaring at Applegate. Applegate smiled, "What's wrong?"

"That was me." Applegate didn't understand. Andrew said, "That was me with the paper route."

$\mathcal{F}$IVE

Applegate's best friend was Elyssia. Elyssia was 75 years old, lived in a Victorian house with three cats, and always wore a string of pearls. They loved to play pinochle together at least once a week. Elyssia had some rather peculiar rules.

Midway into tonight's game, Applegate asked Elyssia, "Are you clumping trubs?"

Elyssia looked at him quizzically. "What?"

Applegate said, "I asked if you were trumping clubs."

"No you didn't."

"I didn't?"

"No. You asked if I was clumping trubs."

"I did?"

"You're starting to talk like me."

"Don't say that!"

Elyssia laughed, "My boyfriend Roy once told me that I had the world's only communicable speech impediment."

"That's all I need."

"Anyway, I'm not trumping clubs."

"I thought you were."

"No. I'm clumping hearts."

Applegate threw down the nine of hearts. "Trump this!"

She played her king of hearts.

"I thought you were trumping them!"

"I lied. How did your tennis date with Tim go?"

Applegate studied his cards. "Tennis?"

"You were supposed to play him yesterday."

"How are you in spades?"

"Loaded."

"That means you're out. And I believe you're out of trump too. Which means my king is safe."

"Would I lie?"

As he played the king of spades, Applegate admitted, "He stood me up."

She took it with her ten of spades and played her ace. "That's a shame."

"That I lost my king?"

"That Tim stood you up."

"Yeah, he's so pretty. I don't know what to do."

"What do you mean?"

"When I see him tomorrow at the YMCA... should I act real angry and risk making him think I'm dependent and clinging, or should I be casual and let him believe I don't mind being stood up, or pretend I forgot, or confront him–"

"And we don't even know if he's gay?"

"All this heartache and he may be straight."

"What does he do for a living?"

"He's an actor and a caterer."

Elyssia said with finality, "He's gay. You could wait and see how he acts. Take your cue from him."

"But I'm angry."

"Then tell him."

"But if I get mad over a simple tennis game, he'll think I'm possessive and desperate and he'll never want to see me again."

"So you don't want to let on to any emotional attachment?"

"Not at this point. I hardly know him. I want to appear cool and independent."

"But open and friendly."

Applegate thought about it. "Open and friendly, but somewhat aloof.

"In order to appear intriguing. To allure from a distance."

"While simultaneously remaining the slightest bit outrageous and uninhibited."

Elyssia laughed. "That should be simple."

"Your deal."

As they put out their meld on the table, Applegate asked, "What's that?"

"What's what?"

"The queen of diamonds and jack of spades. That's not worth anything. A pinochle is a queen of spades and a jack of diamonds."

"This is a semi-pinochle, worth 2 points."

"I never heard of a semi-pinochle."

"Good, you're learning new things from me. I'm a regular Auntie Mame opening doors for you."

"You're more like Sky Masterson stuffing aces up your sleeve. What's the score?"

Elyssia checked the pad of paper and mumbled, "I'm winning, 65 to 29."

"How can that be? You lost the bid in the second hand."

"But I came within two points, and I had both aces of trump. There's a little known rule—"

"I'm sure it's *very* little known."

"Plus before you got here I dealt out a few practice hands—"

Applegate cut in, "And I suppose you played my cards for me?"

"Well, you weren't here, so naturally—"

"Naturally!"

"And that's how you started this game 36 points in the hole."

"From now on, I keep score."

Elyssia sipped her sherry and said, "I hope you're careful when you go sashaying around the gay bars."

"You mean AIDS?"

"No, I mean gay-bashers."

"Don't worry. I always carry this with me." He reached down and showed her the gift she had given him two Christmases ago, a beautiful, pearl-encased, diminutive keychain canister of tear gas.

"Good. Have you ever had to use it?"

"Not so far. People rarely hassle me."

"That's because you don't look like a victim." As she studied her cards she said, "I was watching *Donahue* today. It was about priests getting married."

"I assume you didn't approve."

"I was furious. Why don't they talk about nuns getting married?"

"Nuns?"

"Sure, nuns are people too, you know. Why all this fuss about priests?"

Applegate wondered, "If priests could get married, could they get divorced?"

"And then they mentioned priests going to prostitutes. What I never understood was how they could say prostitution is the world's oldest profession. There had to be other professions first, or how could the prostitutes have gotten paid?"

"A trenchant observation."

"And what about Adam and Eve?"

Applegate asked, "Yeah, what about them?"

"All the Bible says is they were the first couple."

"So?"

"How do we know they weren't dinosaurs?"

"Well…"

$\mathcal{S}$IX

Saturday night at the Blue Gardenia:

"Honestly, I don't know what Kevin got so mad about. He was in one of his intense moods: despair, horror, paranoia… those dark, brooding eyes glowering at me–he's so sexy when he gets like that!–and he said he just had to see *The Boys in the Band.* You know, pre-Stonewall, self-loathing, pariah of mankind, that whole shtick. Said it was the only movie depressing enough to satisfy him. And I mean, he had to see it RIGHT NOW. So I go out at 9:00 o'clock on a Thursday night, pouring rain, and Blockbuster doesn't have *Boys in the Band,* so I get the only other gay flick I could find: *Zorro, the Gay Blade.* Well, when I got home…"

"There he is again."
"I wonder what he wants."
"Is he waiting for someone?"
"I don't think so. He just stands against the wall and watches the videos."

"Then Kevin threw the…"

"You're serious? You've never seen even one Joan Crawford movie?"
"Hey, don't give me that queerer-than-thou attitude."

"No, no, no, all of you are wrong. The worst casting in the history of show business was putting Edward G. Robinson in *The Ten Commandments*. Don't you remember what he sounded like? Picture it: that nasal voice, the sneering, gangster tone… 'So, where's your messiah nyow?'"

"Don't look, there's Steven. I hope he doesn't see–Steven! Darling! I've been searching everywhere for you tonight! I thought you said you'd be at the Vortex!"
"Is that why you're here?"
"Lambie pie! How can you say that? We just came from there. I was combing the dance floor for you…"

"Does he ever talk to anyone?"
"He looks around a lot, but I've never seen him approach anybody."
"Who looks around?"
"We're talking about–"
"He always leaves alone."
"Did you say he's leaving?"
"No, but when he leaves–"
"Who's leaving?"
"No one."
"How long does he stay?"

"Jean-Paul! You look fabulous!" Then, in a whisper to his friend, "He looks like shit!"

"You know, that country-western star who sings, 'You can beat me, kick me, stomp on my face, 'cause I'm your woman.'"

"Last week Terry was talking to him."
"No!"
"Not Terry!"
Derisive laughter.
"Terry the hustler!"
"The guy bought Terry a beer."
"What a chump!"
"He'd be cute if he wasn't so old–sorry, Matthew!"
"You bitch!"
"Who'd be cute? Terry?"
"No, the stranger."
"He's gotta be thirty."
"Anything over 18 is too old for me."

"That's sick."

"When they're teenagers you can get them to do whatever you want."

"You're disgusting."

"You feel the same way with your hustlers. Admit it."

"Give me a break!" Matthew sipped his beer and said to Throckmorton, "I want a man, not a boy."

"You talked to him once, didn't you?"

Matthew smiled. "We discussed his beer."

Throckmorton was delighted to say, "And he shot you down."

"He wasn't interested."

"Maybe he likes 'em young."

Matt responded, "Fuck you."

"Don't be so touchy, sweetie. You know I adore you. In my fashion. But it's time to adjust to your age." Throckmorton hit on the word 'age' venomously. "You have to face the fact that you're approaching the year at which our Lord was crucified. You're a little past the prime of cruising. In case I'm being too subtle–"

Matt said, "I don't consider myself old; I'm chronologically challenged."

"I'm just trying to spare you more heartache. Weirdo over there is obviously looking for a much younger man. You tried once. He chased you away–"

"He didn't exactly chase me. Maybe he was nervous."

"Trust me, Matthew, you're not that scary."

Steven looked at Throckmorton and said, "I'm scared in gay bars. Scared I'll fall asleep listening to all the tired old queens."

Throckmorton glared at him. Paris said to Matthew, "Maybe it's not age at all. Matthew, dear, you're not old." (Those were Paris's words; his tone was more like, "You're not exactly dead… yet.") "Maybe he's not interested in you for other reasons. There could be a veritable plethora of things that turned him off."

"A veritable plethora, huh? Is that anything like a verifiable plethora? Or a versatile plethora?"

Steve interjected, "That hot little number in the Speedos is giving me a vertical plethora."

Paris ignored Steve and said to Matt, "That's okay, go ahead and spew forth your filthy venom, if that makes you feel better. But I swear, I didn't mean to insult you! What I meant was maybe he likes blondes. Maybe he likes 'em short. Maybe you're too intellectual for him."

Matthew studied Applegate in the mirror behind the bar and mused, "Sometimes he looks so detached. Other times, his eyes sparkle."

Throckmorton pleaded dramatically, "Don't do this to yourself. You tried. He said no."

"He didn't say no."

Paris pontificated, "You always throw yourself on these quixotic odysseys."

Matthew responded, "That's a mixed metaphor—"

"At least I didn't say you're embarking up the wrong tree."

Throckmorton warned, "If you're Odysseus, he just might turn out to be a Cyclops."

Paris offered, "That's what I'm looking for tonight: a big one-eye."

Matt was still studying Applegate's face. "He has a nice smile, kind of whimsical. Like he's amused by this place."

Throckmorton snorted. "Amused by the Blue Gardenia? And you call me sick?"

Steve broke in, "Kevin and Alex are having their third fight!"

Matt said, "Let me set my watch. It must be 10:00 o'clock."

Steve laughed, "All I know is, if Alex smashes his glass before midnight, you owe me ten dollars."

"Don't lie to me! You were giving him the eye! I caught you! How dumb do you think I am?!"

Kevin was practically down on one knee as he said, "Alex, baby, I wasn't looking at anything. I was just daydreaming."

"You winked at him!"

"No, I had something in my eye."

"It had nothing to do with your eye! It was something you wanted in your mouth!"

"Alex, sweetheart…"

"That guy in the green tank top? That's Phil. I've known him for years."

"I'd like to know him for about two hours."

"So while I was at Kate's, a dozen roses arrived from her husband. She looked real dreamy and happy and said that whenever she got roses from Eugene, she always spends the next week flat on her back with her legs spread. So I said, honey, why don't you just buy a vase?"

"He never listens to me. He never acts like I have feelings. He treats me like a piece of stone, like a brick in the masonry."

"You're saying he takes you for granite."

"I've been meaning to ask you for years, Throckmorton, what were your parents smoking when they named you?"

"I was giving the safety seminar to a bunch of middle-aged, stuck-up, old, biddy secretaries at this law firm, and I demonstrated how to pop an attacker's eyeballs out of their sockets. Then I said that if a man tries to rape you, grab his testicles and pull as hard as you can. So this one old babe who looks like she hasn't seen a man in 50 years asks, very serious, 'Are you saying that if I yank down hard enough on his testicles, that it will pull his eyeballs back into their sockets?'"

$\mathscr{S}$EVEN

Applegate made his living as a migraine consultant and did volunteer work as a friend-in-need through Wilson Clinic, an institution serving people with AIDS. After going through training, a friend-in-need was assigned to a PWA who had registered at the clinic and requested a friend. The relationship between friend and client was unique for each pair. Some friends-in-need concentrated primarily on giving emotional support, while others occupied themselves with day-to-day responsibilities like cooking and doing laundry for their clients.

Applegate had been assigned to Dutchman for about a year. He heard differing versions of how the nickname "Dutchman" had arisen. One account held that an opera queen fascinated with Wagner's *Flying Dutchman* had imparted that title due to Dutchman's perennial bad luck and his being "light in the loafers." Another rendering maintained that a Baskin-Robbins aficionado had noticed that Dutchman's skin color was identical to Baskin-Robbins' Dark Dutch Chocolate.

Applegate looked around the table at the 9 other friends-in-need gathered for their twice-monthly support group. "It sounds to me like you're all assuming that our clients are going to die."

There was an awkward silence. John said, "In this profession, that's a given."

Applegate felt angry and sad. "But when Dutchman tells me he might live–that he might be able to stay healthy until they find a cure–I believe him."

Rose spoke very quietly. "They might find a cure. But it won't be overnight. And it almost certainly won't be soon enough, or work quick enough, to help the people we work with. All our clients already have AIDS. There's virtually no hope."

Al asked, "Is Dutchman your first client?"

"Yes."

"I'm on my fourth. The first three died. In a span of less than 3 years. You see a lot of death in this job."

"Should I tell Dutchman he's going to die?"

The group became very excited. "No, don't take his hope away."

"Definitely not. Give him all the encouragement you can."

"You never tell a client that. You never play God."

Applegate looked at them all and said, "It's a very fine distinction. I don't want to lie to him. But I don't want to discourage him. I can't tell him he's going to live, because that would give him false hope. But I can't tell him he's going to die, because that would take away his hope and maybe shorten his life."

Jodi, the group leader, said, "It's a tough job. No one said it would be easy. It takes a special person to do what you're doing."

"I think the reason I came tonight–the reason I felt I had to be here… I'm just beginning to realize that I've been deluding myself. Until this week, I never really considered that Dutchman would die. I suppose I'm real naive. But I didn't think that far ahead. I just wanted to help."

*E*IGHT

Dutchman provocatively said, "I got this fine-looking man coming over tomorrow."

Applegate asked, "A date?"

"No, to look at my lamp."

"That porcelain nightmare with the cherubs?"

"Yeah, it's broken. It takes special handling."

"How much is he charging you?"

"Seventy dollars for the house call, then twenty dollars an hour. One hour minimum." When Dutchman saw the expression on Applegate's face, he explained, "I know it's expensive, but it's got to be done."

Dutchman could barely pay his rent each month. He lived on Social Security, money from Calvin, and handouts from friends and fellow church-goers. Applegate was disturbed that Dutchman would pay so much money just to fix a decorative lamp, but it wasn't his role to lecture Dutchman. He also thought to the time last month when Dutchman had paid fifty dollars to have a carpet professionally cleaned. They did a good job, but when you're living hand-to-mouth you simply can't afford such non-necessities.

Applegate and Dutchman sat on the grass, looking out at Lake Michigan. It was too early in the spring for sailboats, so the lake was vast and placid. New sprouts on the tree above them were green and stark against the weathered bark and barren branches.

Dutchman said, "I saw my sister last week."

"Val?"

"Yeah. After church on Sunday, she invited me over for lunch. She acts like she doesn't know I have the virus. But whenever she sees me, she asks me how do I feel and where was I when she called and how come I don't have a job."

"She's not really interested?"

"She's just prying 'cause she's nosy. She wants to call our mama and tell her I'm sick."

"It sounds like you don't get a lot of support from your family."

"I don't get no support. Sunday night when we were eating, my little nephew goes to take a bite from my plate, and Val went nuts. She like screamed, 'No! Don't touch that!'"

"She's afraid her son could get AIDS from a plate?"

Dutchman didn't answer for several moments. Applegate looked to the horizon at a cloud suspended over the vast expanse of water.

"It's like when we were all drinking beer at Yvonne's house. I put down my can. Simon, my brother-in-law, put his right by mine. When he went to drink, he forgot which beer was his. He went and got a new one 'cause he wouldn't take the chance of drinking from the same can as me."

"People are scared. They're also stupid sometimes. They don't do it to hurt you."

Dutchman shook his head. "Simon never did like me. Before he married Val he would talk about me, calling me his girlfriend's punk brother."

"Punk?"

"Gay. You know what else Val said? She said that I made her kids sick. When they came down with colds, she said it was my virus that made them sick."

"Even though she pretends she doesn't know you're HIV positive?"

"They all know. They just don't talk about it."

"It's possible you gave her kids a cold, if you had one. But it's a lot more likely that they would make you sick than you them."

"My ma called from New York."

"How was that?"

Dutchman smiled. "She kept asking me questions about why do I sound so weak and how come Val tells her I lost weight."

"Did you ever think of forcing the issue? Just coming out and saying, 'Mom, I have AIDS'?"

"They don't want to hear it. They know."

"Who are your friends?"

Dutchman thought a while. "My friends? I guess it's the guys you met at the party."

"I liked them all a lot."

With uncharacteristic bitterness, Dutchman said, "None of them visited me in the hospital."

"When you had PCP?"

"None of them. I didn't have any visitors."

"What about Calvin?"

"No, he had to go to Michigan to stay with his sick aunt."

"Even though you were sick too?"

Dutchman was lost in thought several moments. Finally he laughed and said, "He's mad at us."

"At both of us?"

Dutchman laughed. "Yeah."

"Why?"

"He don't understand why we don't include him when we go out like this. He wants to come along."

"We don't have just a friendship, Dutchman. We have a professional relationship."

"That's what I told him. But you know Calvin. He's still mad. He got real mad after you left the party. You should have seen it."

"Who was he mad at?"

"Everyone. He started in on Yvonne because she hadn't come around for a month and she didn't bring me a gift. He's yelling at her, she's screaming at him. Then Philip tried to get between them, and Calvin turned on him, telling him he knows that Phil and I are screwing behind his back."

"Calvin is jealous of you and Philip?"

"He talks about every man I meet like I'm fucking them. He leaves the apartment sometimes, and I know he's waiting across the street to see if any men come over. He thinks I'm fucking Ogden."

Applegate laughed. "So he caused a big scene at the party?"

"He always starts a fight when he drinks. He hates Ogden because I tell him all the shit Ogden says about him."

"What does Ogden say about Calvin?"

"That he's jealous and a drunk and not good enough for me."

Applegate was astonished. "You told Calvin that Ogden said that?"

"Sure, I don't give a fuck. They hate each other. Ogden just wants me for himself."

"You have two men chasing after you? What's your secret?"

Dutchman laughed and said, "Twelve big ones! That's my secret!" There was a long pause before he said, "I think I'm gonna throw Calvin out."

"Really? Why?"

"He keeps saying we're lovers. I told him we're just friends. Every time we have a party he gets drunk and accuses me of fucking all these men behind his back. He thinks you and me are screwing; that's the real reason he wants to come along."

"And you don't like the constant accusations?"

"I told him to knock it off or I'll throw his ass out. I mean it."

"Could you get along without him?"

"It would be tough. He does all the housework. And he gives me a hundred dollars a month." He was lost in thought for several minutes and then asked, "What do you think?"

Applegate said, "I don't know. I don't know him at all. I think what's important is how you feel about him. Are you living with him because you feel like he enriches your life? Or because you need the money?"

"I got a lot of men after my ass. I was walking down the street last week, and this one bitch asked me if I wanted to fuck him."

"A stranger?"

"Yeah a stranger. He said I could fuck him for ten dollars. He was cupping his dick and fingering himself and asking if I want to take him home and fuck him. I said, 'Honey, how do you know what I got? I could have the AIDS.' And he said, 'That's what rubbers are for.' I said, 'Bitch, rubbers break.' He said, 'That's the chance you take.' So he followed me down the street, asking if I want to fuck him for ten dollars, how about eight, how about five and what do I have in my ice box, five dollars and some meat, a chicken leg!"

Applegate said, "Maybe you should give me lessons in how you walk."

$\mathcal{N}$INE

At Little Jim's on Halsted, a venerable Chicago bar which has been in business longer than most Chicago gay men have been alive, a group of Thursday afternoon regulars were arranged in front of the TV monitor, critiquing the latest offering from Crotch 'n' Jock Studios.

"Come on! You need a little lube first!"

"They're using oil. Can't you see how shiny his ass is?"

"Where did it come from? They're in an empty warehouse."

"You just have to accept it. It's called the willing suspension of disbelief."

"Speaking of suspension, look at that! Look at that! I don't demand much from a porno star, but I do think that they should keep it hard."

"Judging from how dilated his pupils are, I think we're lucky his dick isn't up inside him."

"Is that supposed to be sexy?"

"Which?"

"The demented look."

"He does appear to be a little… neanderthal."

"With a dick that big, I don't care if he's a fucking gorilla."

"His dick isn't really as big as it looks. They do it with mirrors."

"You should get one of those mirrors!"

"Who is this guy anyway?"

"Some upstart newcomer."

"I prefer the classics."

"Yeah, like Jacques Hardoné."

For the benefit of the uninitiated, Jacques Hardoné (pronounced "Zhack Har-doe-NAY" but often perverted to "Jock HARD-on") is one of the megastars of gay porno. In a profession where most performers brag of being exclusively a top, Jacques flaunts his preference for being bottom. Once, after ingesting a prodigious amount of illegal drugs, he was quoted as saying, "The enduring ontological paradox of the porn industry is that most of the tops are fucking assholes."

Applegate, sitting a few stools away from the group and watching the video with them, finally said something. "Jacques Hardoné is my favorite. Know what I love about him?"

The five or six men gathered at the bar all spoke at once, offering various body parts which might answer the question. Applegate continued, "No, what I love about Jacques is that he talks while he's fucking. I saw *The Best of Jacques Hardoné* and he was with a dozen different guys, and with each one, he kept up a steady line of chatter."

One man, sitting aloof and stiffly sipping a glass of red wine, raised an eyebrow and asked, "What, pray tell, does one chatter about when one is committing the act of darkness?"

"His favorite line is, 'You like putting that big dick up my ass, don't you?'"

The man looked askance at Applegate. "Did he manage to work it often into the conversation?"

"Well, in this one clip where he was with an auto mechanic, he was asking, 'You like that hard cock up my ass, don't you, grease monkey?' Then when he was with a Roman gladiator, it was, 'You like shoving that big dick up my ass, don't you, helmet head?' Then when he was with a vegetarian eskimo—"

"I think I get the general drift."

"But at least he talks. Those other guys at most grunt now and then. A lot of times when Jacques asks, 'You like that, don't you?', they ignore him. So he'll repeat, and maybe they'll snort. Then he'll say, 'Tell me! Tell me you like my sweet ass!' And maybe, just maybe, the other guy will say, 'I like the sweet ass.' I don't know why they're so reticent."

"Porno stars aren't hired for their acting ability."

"Come on, they have to have some talent. I mean, a pretty face and a big dick can open a lot of doors for you, but once you walk in the door, there are a thousand other guys with pretty faces and big dicks—"

"Just where is this door?"

All the men were strangers to Applegate. One said, "I like the works of William Higgins."

"What's he been in?"

"No, he's a director. Very erotic and understated. He has a movie where all the action takes place under a silk sheet."

"You don't see anything?"

"You see everything. The material is sheer, so you get a clear picture of what's going on, but it's like it's in soft focus."

Applegate's eyes glazed over as he said, with reverent awe, "That sounds really nice."

"He has another movie with four or five guys swimming naked in a pool. All the sex takes place underwater. Innocent and natural. Kind of has a boy scouts quality. The guys seem to be really enjoying themselves. And they all stay hard."

Applegate said, "I saw a movie where one guy was rimming the other, and the rimmee was saying, 'You eat good ass.' Now, I thought that was a great way to put it. What he means, of course, is 'You eat ass well.' But by saying 'You eat good ass,' it seems to make it a joint effort, like my ass is good and you eat it well."

Applegate moved down a few stools to be with the group. Someone said, "I saw a great movie the other day. Here's the plot… it was raining out, and when this guy got to his friend's house, the friend said, 'Hey, you're soaked to the skin.' Then he says, 'You better get out of those wet things before you catch your death of cold.'"

Applegate, laughing, asked, "That's the whole plot?"

"Well, that's the plot proper. But the denouement takes an hour!"

"My favorite line is from *Butt Boys In Space*, when he says, 'Make it rage like a photon torpedo!'"

"I think they should have awards for porno flicks. You know, with categories like 'Best Actor in a Supporting Role', 'Best Actor in a Supporter'…"

"They do! I swear to God I read it somewhere they do have awards for porno!"

"You know what really gets me hot is watching Pee Wee Herman."

"You mean all those gorgeous guys he's got running around the playhouse?"

"Yeah! Like Ricardo with the muscles who never wears a shirt!"

"Or Cowboy Curtis!"

There was a collective sigh and the room temperature rose noticeably. "Yeah, Cowboy Curtis!"

"I used to tape it every Saturday morning, so if I struck out Saturday night, at least I knew I had Cowboy Curtis waiting for me in my bedroom."

"I've always wondered about Jombie. That girl wears a lot of makeup!"

"And that hat!"

"The guy's a screaming queen! Listen carefully next time. Whenever he comes on, he's supposed to say, 'Wish? Wish? Did someone say wish?' But he really says, 'Swish? Swish?'"

"Get out of here!"

"I'm serious!"

After another half hour Applegate rose and said, "Well, I gotta go now. I have a client to see. But it's been fun."

After he walked out the door, one of the men turned to another and said, "He left without telling us what Jacques said to the vegetarian eskimo."

$\mathcal{T}$EN

With a name like Matthew Bumpers, you learn to maintain a sense of humor. Matt, pushing 33, held a Bachelor's degree in English and had spent several years pursuing liberal-arts-graduate type jobs: middle-management or creative-trainee positions in advertising firms and art galleries. Then, at the age of 30, he unexpectedly inherited $100,000. He used the money to open a used and rare book store.

Matt's store, Bumpers' Books on Broadway, was very successful. Matt found out that the real money in used/rare books was in mail order. He spent his days at the store talking with customers or making an occasional sale, but the real work was in writing up catalog entries, researching trade journals, poring over "books wanted" listings, mailing out bids and filling incoming orders. He was successful enough to have both a part-time employee and a flexible schedule which allowed him to schmooze when regulars would come by to discuss politics and religion. Never an overly-ambitious man, Matt lived comfortably, traveled frequently, and knew his way around Chicago's theater district. Unfortunately, he usually saw plays alone.

The store always smelled wonderful from the various coffees—hazelnut, amaretto, jamoca—he brewed for his customers. Matt enjoyed debate and loved to listen to the fascinating conversation of his customers.

Winston was wearing torn jeans and an Indigo Girls T-shirt. He adjusted his wire-rim glasses for the thousandth time as he lectured Carlyle, "You never

call it sexual preference. The correct term is sexual orientation. Sexual preference implies that we can change it anytime we want, that it's not part of our
essence, and that makes us vulnerable to attacks by bigots who want to wipe us
out and say we're gay because we choose to be."

With a snort, Carlyle leaned back in his chair Clarence Darrow-style and
stuck his thumbs under his suspenders. "That is so stupid that I don't believe
even you believe it. There's nothing rigid about orientation. During the day
one side of the earth is oriented towards the sun, then at night the other side is.
And even that changes by the minute. Compass needles are oriented to the
north, but a magnet can throw them off. Preference is a lot more permanent
than orientation. Besides, who you choose to have sex with throughout your
life is always a matter of inclination and mood, which is constantly changing
within each individual."

"You don't understand! Preference means–"

"The same thing as orientation when you apply it to human behavior.
They're synonyms! Besides, we can't be defining ourselves on the defensive,
choosing our name based on what some asshole will say–"

"You're playing right into their hands!"

"You're being a fucking idiot!"

"You're insensitive!"

"You're nuts!"

Well, usually it was fascinating conversation. On days like today, Matthew
wished he was still stocking the shelves at the Art Institute gift store.

Carlyle glanced through the newspaper and called out, "Hey Matt, did you
see you've been denounced again in the *Windy City Times?*"

"That letter calling me a Nazi? Yeah. Jesus, they're blowing it all out of pro-
portion."

Winston asked, "Which embroglio is it this week?"

Matt turned to him. "Look, all I said was that men are not the enemy of
women. This letter makes it sound like I was promoting rape. I was at this lesbian coffee-house where there was a poster for a women's self-defense course. It
showed a smiling, middle-aged white man in a suit, with arrows pointing to different parts of his body and captions like 'gouge out his eyes', 'kick him in the
groin', 'stomp on his instep'–"

Winston interrupted, "But that's basic self-defense. What's wrong with that?"

"I said in my editorial that the poster would be perceived by the average
man–which in no sense includes you!–as hostile, and it fosters the idea that lesbians hate men. The poster could have used an androgynous figure rather than
a male, or the figure could have been a woman."

"But women don't attack other women! Of course it was a male figure!"

"They didn't need to use a figure at all!"

Carlyle asked Winston, "What if it had been a poster put out by the military, showing hetero soldiers how to fend off sexual advances from gay soldiers?"

Matt offered, "Yeah, with captions like 'kick him in the spandex', 'stomp on his Doc Martens'–"

"'Muss up his hair!'"

"The column I wrote was a plea for understanding between gays and lesbians. I gave a half-dozen examples of male insensitivity to lesbians, and one example of lesbian insensitivity to men. But everyone's reacting like I assassinated Betty Friedan."

Matt re-read the letter in the *Windy City Times*. He used to be active in political groups. Ten years ago, a controversy like this would have roused his passions. He could recall when he would be part of a committee presenting a position paper. They could argue for hours over whether a certain clause should end with a period or a semicolon; Matt, himself, would be spokesman for one side or the other. It all seemed very important.

But while he loved defending his ideas, he deeply resented the vicious personal attacks which had become common in gay politics. The last several meetings he had attended had resulted in his fending off endless charges of racism, sexism, fascism, elitism. It seemed particularly perverse, since all through his childhood he had been reviled as a "sissy" and a "nigger-lover" in the blue-collar neighborhood where he grew up.

It made Matt wonder what it meant to be gay. Was it meetings and discussion? Was it making love? Was it bars and dancing? Was it personals and telephone sex?

Matt looked outside at a tree in front of his store, bursting with green on this June afternoon. The summer heat had been sweltering for the last two weeks, but today a cool breeze was coming straight off Lake Michigan. It brought with it the smell of new-mown grass and images of a russet, autumn day many years ago when Matt and his high school friend Roger had ditched classes and gone to the forest preserves.

They had found their way to a secluded, mossy pond deep in the woods and were dangling their bare feet in the cool water. Roger was dreamily strumming his guitar and singing something about a storm threatening when Matt suddenly realized that it was a folk version of "Gimme Shelter" by the Rolling Stones. Without the drums and the driving bass, Matt hadn't even recognized the melody. As Roger's tenor voice caressed the words, the song took on an ethereal quality.

Multicolored leaves were falling from the trees, and a bright orange leaf landed in Roger's hair. Matt leaned over and blew the leaf back into the air. He watched it somersault in front of Roger's face and float down to the surface of the water. Matt lay back and let all the sensations of the moment wash over him… the aroma of drying leaves, the water-splashed rocks in the sun, the celestial music, the warmth of Roger's leg next to his…

Matt knew the time had come to reveal his secret. Perhaps it was their physical contact which gave him the courage. Perhaps it was the line in Roger's song about love being "just a kiss away" that gave him hope. Matt sat up and awkwardly blurted out, "I love you. I'm gay and I'm in love with you."

Roger stopped singing but continued to gently strum the guitar. Rather than look at Matt, Roger studied the bright orange leaf which continued to bob on the surface of the pond. It was probably the most vulnerable moment of Matt's life, and yet he felt completely at peace. The musical notes seemed to take on physical form, dancing around them like fireflies, bursting like soap bubbles, isolating them from the rest of the world.

Neither spoke for a long time. Matt relaxed in a warm bath of the caressing, forgiving chords. Finally Roger turned to Matt, reached his hand around the back of Matt's neck and pulled him close until their foreheads touched. He looked into Matt's eyes and whispered, "We're friends for life, buddy." Matt broke into a big, goofy grin as his eyes blazed with naked hero worship. Roger laughed and tousled Matt's hair.

Roger's response was that simple. That perfect. Friendship was all that Roger could offer and, in some paradoxical way, it was everything that Matt desired from him. All he wanted was to be in Roger's presence, to hear him play the guitar and sing about storms and kisses and other boyhood mysteries.

Roger was always more daring than Matt, more committed and passionate. He died a few years after that afternoon. Though Matt couldn't account for the feeling, he was certain that Roger's death had been violent.

Matt didn't like to tell the story, because he didn't have any explanation to go with it. No one knew exactly what happened to Roger. After graduation from high school, Roger had gone off to college in another state. He and Matt gradually grew apart. Over the years, Matt began to hear rumors. Someone claimed he saw Roger in New York, looking ragged and confused. Another friend claimed Roger was a street person in San Francisco.

Calls to Roger's parents confirmed only that they didn't know where he was. Finally, his body was found in a cheap hotel in Los Angeles. No one knew why. No one knew if it was murder, suicide, or overdose. Roger's parents refused to talk about it. They had a quiet, private funeral to which none of Roger's friends were invited.

Why was he thinking so much of Roger these days? Something kept reminding him, some incident or some face he had seen recently… a face like Roger's, full of curiosity tinged with fear, full of life shadowed by sorrow. Some new image had touched him, but just now he couldn't place where he had seen it. It had to do with the hesitant longing of first desire, the shy boldness of

Roger's friendship for Matt.

There was another story in the paper, about a federal judge who was censured for referring to gay men as queers. Matt was pleased that the judge was reprimanded. Then he read the judge's defense: there is a gay group, Queer Nation, that uses the word in its title. How could the judge have known the word was offensive when gays themselves use it?

The judge had a point. We do refer to ourselves as queer. The newspaper Matt was reading used queer and gay synonymously. It was voguish to say, "I'm queer." So how could the judge be expected to know?

He came across an article on Wilson Clinic. Now there was an idea. They were always looking for volunteers, and it would be a real challenge to work with people with AIDS. Surely there couldn't be much controversy about an organization whose sole purpose is to bring comfort to the sick.

He read some of the article. It was a blistering attack. It seems the president of Wilson Clinic happens to be female. The writer was saying that this insults all gay men by implying that we can't take care of ourselves, that we need a female to nurture us.

Matt threw down the paper in disgust. At one time, he had lived for such debate. Now it all seemed pointless and overdone. At some point we simply have to stop debating and get on with the business of being queer. The idea behind eliminating racial or gender prejudice was to allow us to love each other. But it never seemed to happen. It never got solved or got done; it always turned back on itself and began all over again.

It had been a big day in Matt's life when the *Wall Street Journal* had announced its new policy of describing homosexual men as gay. Up until then, it would only refer to them as homosexual. Now we were back to queer, but even that was a controversy.

The atmosphere was different. Ten years ago, debating semicolon-versus-period as fiercely as they were now debating queer-versus-gay, there had been a feeling of trust and community. At the end of the debate, no matter how heated, they had all gone out together for a few beers and some serious dishing. Now it seemed vicious and unforgiving. If you're not with them, you're the enemy. There is no loyal opposition.

Matt felt he had to do something primal and certain. He got a sudden inspiration.

"Hey, Winston! Carlyle! What do you say to a jack-off party? My place, tonight?"

Carlyle said, "Jack-off party? God, we haven't done that in years. Sure, I'll be there."

Winston proclaimed, "Typical white male! TYPICAL white male. Now do you see what's wrong with the gay movement? Why we need more women and people of color in positions of leadership? Lesbians would never think of attending anything as exploitative and impersonal as a jack-off party. Asians are too inventive to settle for something so childish. Blacks have more self-respect—"

Carlyle said, "I'm glad you new-age radicals don't indulge in stereotypes!"

Matt said to Winston, "I take it you're not coming?"

"Well, no, I didn't exactly say… I assume you're serving a buffet?"

"There'll be plenty of liquid protein available. I'll have to go to the store to get a bunch of shopping bags for everyone to put their clothes in. I better make sure I have enough sheets to cover all the chairs. I think I can count on around a dozen guys."

Carlyle offered, "Let me get the bags. Last time they all said True Value Hardware across the front."

"I thought that was a nice touch. Real butch. And I'll need to go to the video store for some Jacques Hardoné—"

Winston asked, "Will you have any films featuring porno stars of color?"

"Porno stars of color?"

Carlyle said, "Please, I'll get the shopping bags. Something fitting for the occasion, like Fannie Mae's or Bloomingdale's."

Matt reminisced, "I haven't been back to Bloomingdale's since I broke up with Clarence two years ago."

"Ah, yes, the famous Bloomingdale's screaming match. Ever since you first told me that story I've been convinced that it's the only way to dump a lover. What was it? He insulted your taste in pottery?"

Matt laughed, "No, he picked up this hideous salad bowl and was raving about how divine it would be at our next dinner party. I looked at it and told him that he had garage sale taste. Next thing I know, there's this explosion of glass—"

"I bet he gave you *such a look*!"

Winston declared sullenly, "A bunch of white male faggots are going to jerk off tonight—"

Roger's face that afternoon—the soft, understanding eyes, the lips parted to reveal pearly teeth, the chocolate brown skin—flashed through Matt's mind as he smiled and said, "That's what it means to be gay in the nineties!"

$\mathcal{E}$LEVEN

Guildenstern crouched forward. He was panting as he asked, "Now?"

Rosencrantz cautioned him. "No, not now! Wait till he takes his shoes off. Otherwise he might step on you."

"Can't he step on us in his bare feet?"

Rosencrantz snorted derisively and said, "This crybaby? He couldn't stand the squish."

"Why's he taking so long?"

Rosencrantz studied Applegate for several seconds. Finally he said, "He looks depressed."

"He's distracted?"

Rosencrantz seemed concerned. "I'd say so."

Guildenstern chortled. "So he'll really scream, huh!?"

Rosencrantz continued to study Applegate. "I don't know. Maybe we should leave him alone tonight. He looks like he's having man trouble."

"It's been weeks since we blitzed him."

Rosencrantz was amused by Guildenstern's new-found excitement. "This is quite a change in you. The first time we did this, you were terrified. I practically had to pull your wings off to get you in here. Now you're a regular fiend."

Guildenstern smacked his little cockroach lips and sneered, "You converted me. Applegate is the most fun I've had since that dead cat in the vacant apartment."

"That was a party! Maggots make delightful companions, don't they?"

"So when he takes his shoes off, I run over his toes, right?"

"I don't know."

"That was the plan."

Rosencrantz looked at Applegate and said, "Maybe we should... tell you what, why don't you hide under his toothpaste? That way, when he goes to pick it up, you can run across the sink–"

"It would be more fun to actually touch him."

Rosencrantz felt a stab of pity for Applegate. "I don't feel like it tonight. Let's just leave, okay?"

"Come on!"

"Seriously, if we go too far, he might move. A run for the wall once a month is one thing. But actually touching him... he just might move out altogether. Let's go play in the Roach Away, then call it a night."

"I want some action!"

Suddenly Rosencrantz's antennae stood up straight in the air. His pity was quickly being replaced by passion. "Here he comes..." Rosencrantz hesitated a moment before he could catch his breath to add, ". . . barefoot!"

Guildenstern wriggled and squirmed and said, "Yeah! Yeah! Let me know..."

Now Rosencrantz's pity returned. "I'm not sure about this." Rosencrantz caught a whiff of bare-feet aroma. His antennae wagged wildly. He unconsciously leaned forward on four sets of tiptoes. His wings trembled.

Guildenstern panted, "He's almost here."

Rosencrantz's heart was racing. He saw Applegate's bare toes stop just inches from him. They were pink. The nails were shiny. They flexed slightly. They were just a half-foot away. Rosencrantz, swept away by the thrill of it all, said, "Oh, what the hell. Let's both do it! A double whammy! NOW!!!!"

$\mathscr{T}$WELVE

Jerry Applegate
Migraine Consultant

You've probably never heard the term "migraine consultant" before. As far as I know, I'm the only person who offers the service.

I suffered severe migraines, usually daily, for 15 years, from the time I was 12 years old until I was 27. I've overcome them completely, and now I help other sufferers do the same.

I am not a medical professional, nor am I a psychologist. My only training is a bachelor's degree in Philosophy from a small liberal arts college, and a certificate in massage therapy from the East-West School of Massage Therapy.

I am a consultant. I use my experience to help my clients work out a pain-management program. In our initial interview, I evaluate my client, make recommendations, and describe my personal reactions to the therapies I recommend. Then we meet again in a week and see how things worked out. It usually takes six to eight 50-minute sessions to establish a satisfactory pain-management program, after which we may have occasional follow-up sessions as needed.

The recommendations I make do not come out of a textbook; they come from my own struggle of 15 years. For some clients, I'll suggest acupuncture. Others may need psychotherapy. I always insist on a program of exercise and sound nutrition. I have a working relationship with local chiropractors, nutritionists, hypnotists, health food stores, homeopathic pharmacists, 12-step programs, M.D.s and psychologists. When appropriate, I provide massage therapy. There is no extra charge for this.

Overcoming your migraines will not be easy. The first thing I will ask you to do is to turn over all your painkilling medication to me. Then I'll ask you to sign a form which I will send to your doctor, requesting that s/he cease prescribing all narcotics. I know from experience how terrifying this step is; I took it myself. But if you aren't willing to stop all narcotics, you are not ready to let go of the migraines, and there is nothing I can do to help you.

Applegate always smiled when he read that part. Indeed, all his clients would turn over their pills and sign the form. But virtually every one failed to inform Applegate that they had half a dozen doctors prescribing for them; they always held onto their secret sources.

Applegate had done the same for years. It was the easiest thing in the world to see a new doctor and come away with a prescription for a week's supply of codeine, along with 2 refills. Applegate was always amazed at how irresponsible M.D.s were when it came to dispensing narcotics. Most would cut him off after a month or so, but there were always hundreds more he could visit. With his medical insurance paying the tab, it was a good scam. Until Applegate got serious about overcoming the problem.

Someone once asked Applegate, "How do you know if it's really migraines, or if it's just regular headaches?"

Applegate had responded, "If it's migraines, in the first session the client sooner or later will say something like, 'the pain gets so intense sometimes that I actually wish I could die.'"

"How many of the people who come to you say that?"

Applegate paused before answering, "Every single one."

*T*HIRTEEN

Jacques walked into the room wearing faded jeans, a plaid flannel shirt and a sensual pout, carrying a six-pack of imported beer. He took off his hard-hat, looked Applegate up and down and whistled. "Oooooo, baby, you sure look fine tonight."

"So do you!"

"Oh, honey, I couldn't wait to get home to you so you could make love to my ass. Make love to my ass with that sweet cock of yours."

Applegate responded, "That's the only kind I've got!"

Jacques began to unbutton his shirt. "All day long I could feel your stiff prick up my ass. All day long, every time I took a step, I could feel you in me." As he removed the shirt altogether he said, "I hope you don't mind that I'm a little sweaty. I been working all day, and I'm one sweaty hunk o' man. Can you smell my man sweat?"

Applegate was surprised to realize he could. "You smell fine and manly to me, Jacques."

Jacques unzipped his jeans. "I'll just get out of these hot, sweaty clothes and jump in the shower. Do you want to shower with me, sweet-stuff?" Jacques pursed his lips and whispered desperately, "I been dreaming all day long of seeing your sweet, sassy ass in the shower. I can't wait any longer. Please! Don't keep me waiting!"

Applegate whimpered, "No! No! I won't!"

"'Cause it's hard when I want a man… as bad as I want you."

"I'm hard too…"

Jacques, stripped to his jockey shorts, arched his body and pleaded, "Come to me now!"

Applegate nearly fell out of bed. When he noticed that his glass was empty, he pressed the "pause" button and Jacques froze in mid-leer. Applegate returned with a fresh beer and pressed "play" to resume viewing.

With an impish, innocent grin, Jacques asked Applegate, "Will you give it to me, baby? You know what I like! Can I have it? Come on, joy-chunks, unzip those pants…"

A few hours later, as Applegate lay asleep, he was awakened by the telephone. The voice he heard was smiling. "Hi, Applegate. Do you know who this is?"

"Jacques? Jacques Hardoné?"

"None other."

"What's going on? Are you having a migraine?"

"No, nothing like that. But you know I like to see you when I'm in town. And I don't just mean professionally. Can I come over?"

"How soon can you get here?"

Jacques materialized at the foot of Applegate's bed.

He smiled his Jacques Hardoné smile and said, "I thought I'd drop by to see how you liked my video. Was it… hot enough for you?"

"Oh, Jocko, of course. You're the best."

"You like the sweet ass, don't you?"

"Sure, who wouldn't–"

"You'd like to stick your big hard dick up that ass, wouldn't you?"

"Later maybe. Jacques, can you tell me about relationships?"

"Sure. The guy on the bottom receives, and–"

"There's something I want…"

Jacques lay on the bed, arching his back and lazily rubbing his groin. "You want this big dick in your mouth, don't you, Applegate?"

"Why do you always say *that* ass and *this* dick?"

Jacques was startled. He sat up and asked, "What?!"

"I mean, they are yours, aren't they?"

"I don't get it."

"Why don't you say *my* dick and *my* ass? Why is it always *that* dick? You make it sound so impersonal."

"You mean like I only relate to other gay men as a body?"

"Exactly!"

Jacques asked, "Do you know why you were able to see that in me?"

"Why?"

"Because you're the same way."

"No, I really want–"

"When you're in a gay bar, why are you so afraid?"

Applegate fumbled with his words. "Well, in a gay bar… I'm out of my element. I don't know what's expected of me. I'm so intimidated–"

"By all the beautiful bodies."

Applegate thought about it. "Yeah, they all look so pretty. It really throws me."

"Because they look so beautiful, you assume that all they want in return is another beautiful body. And you don't think you measure up."

"Well, no, I'm not that attractive. I'm 29 years old."

"See what I mean? You only relate to other gay men as a body. You think you have to be young and svelte and a Tom Cruise clone in order to interest them. You never even stop to consider that they might like talking with you because you're interesting."

"I think beautiful people tend to be attracted to other beautiful people."

Jacques laughed and shook his head. "I was wrong. You're not like me; you're a lot worse. Because you've got it in your head that you're ugly. You really believe that you're hideous, when, take it from me, you could co-star in my next flick. Honest."

"No one ever approaches me."

"What about that guy who asked you what kind of beer you were drinking?"

"Well, yeah…"

"And you ran away. You push them away, Applegate. They're not ignoring you. But you're not ready."

Jacques picked up the remote control for the VCR. "You always control me with this. I'll show you how I can turn that around." He punched a few buttons and placed the unit against Applegate's chest.

Applegate began to rise off the bed. He looked around nervously. Jacques said, "Just relax. I have a little surprise for you. You'll like it."

As he approached the ceiling Applegate said, "I don't know about this!"

Jacques purred, "Trust me."

Applegate was now levitating on his back six feet above the floor, his ceiling just two feet from his face. Jacques said, "Put your arms out in front of you to the wall. I'm gonna give you a little shove. When you get up against the wall, push yourself backwards. Be sure you don't hit your head. And when you push, do it real gentle." He leered at Applegate. "Real slow and gentle. Okay?" His smile was cocky.

Applegate was starting to relax. "Whatever you say."

Jacques grabbed Applegate's waist with both hands and very softly sent him gliding to the wall. He added a slight twist so that Applegate spiraled forward.

Applegate looked around as he floated ever so slowly. He tried to remember what flying signifies in dreams.

As Applegate rebounded off the wall and glided back, Jacques said, "Now get ready. Here goes!" With that Jacques leapt on top of him. Holding him close, he gave Applegate a passionate kiss. The two men levitated near the ceiling, coasting backward, rolling over and over in each other's arms. Applegate didn't need a degree in psychology to know the significance of their corkscrew motion.

OURTEEN

♩

Chardonnay was one of Applegate's more interesting migraine clients. What she lacked in determination she made up for in… actually, Applegate wasn't sure what her strong suit was.

"Do you like this outfit on me?"

Applegate looked across his desk at Chardonnay and said, "Yes, it's very nice."

Chardonnay was puzzled. "I get a lot of compliments on it. I don't know why."

Applegate had been through this before. He wanted to yell, "You get compliments on your clothes because you always ask everyone how they like them," but he knew from experience that she was sincere. "Anyway, I was saying that with some clients, I recommend acupuncture–"

"I threw up this morning."

Applegate was concerned. "I see. Do you know why?"

"No. I throw up a lot in the morning."

"What were you doing last night?"

Chardonnay was lost in thought. She suddenly looked directly at Applegate and asked, "What?"

"I asked what you were doing last night."

"I was out with Eric, my gay friend."

"What did you two do?"

"We went bar-hopping. We always go to gay bars. Everyone talks to me."

"Is that so?"

"Yeah, we walk into a bar and everyone looks at us. It's because I'm so beautiful and Eric's so tall. He's six foot two. He comes by his heightness in a heretical fashion."

Applegate stroked his chin and asked, "Heretical? You mean he made a pact with the devil?"

"No, heretical. By heredity. He got it from his parents."

"How silly of me."

"And all the gay boys love my hair. They come up to me and tell me how wonderful it is. They all want to touch it."

"Were you drinking last night?"

In sudden exasperation she asked, "What do you think? We had about three pitchers each of Long Island Iced Tea."

"Well, maybe that's why you were throwing up this morning."

She asked, very seriously, "Do you think that could be it?"

Applegate said, "Well, yes, alcohol does that to people. Especially migraine sufferers."

"You told me vodka was alright."

"I said that if you're going to drink anything, you're better off with vodka or gin because they don't contain congeners which can worsen a hangover and cause a migraine. Red wine is the worst for most migraine sufferers, followed closely by whiskey. I've also had clients express absolute horror for the effects of champagne."

Chardonnay looked dreamy and said, "Champagne tastes so good going down… and so nasty coming up."

"I'm not just speaking from my own experience; alcohol and chocolate are the two most notorious nutritional causes of migraines."

"I was sweating when I woke up this morning. And shaking."

"Sounds bad. What did you do?"

"I went to the bathroom to lie down for a while. I was hyperventilating and I couldn't breathe."

"Both at once, huh?"

"The worst part was I could still taste the butter."

"The butter?"

"That I had last night."

"You had butter last night?"

"When I got home. I ate about a stick."

"You ate a stick of butter?"

Chardonnay seemed somewhat defiant. "Yeah."

"You just sat down with a knife and fork and stick of–"

"No!" Again she was exasperated. "No, don't be silly. I put it on a piece of cinnamon toast."

"An entire stick?"

"Well, I spread it kind of thick…"

"Of course. How stupid of me."

"And, man, when I was on the bathroom floor, that's all I could taste. Plus all I had in the refrigerator for breakfast was ice cream."

"Ice cream?"

"My philosophy is that if you're going to have nothing but something in your refrigerator, it may as well be ice cream."

"I can't challenge that."

"I decided I'm quitting dental hygiene school."

"Why?"

"I've told you before that I hate it."

"How many years have you been studying it?"

"About five."

Applegate raised an eyebrow. "Five? Isn't that a long time?"

"Well, I'm in the 15-year program."

"Fifteen years?"

"That's a joke."

"Oh, I see."

Chardonnay declared, "I'm going to start school in the fall."

"But not in dental hygiene?"

"No, in mathematics."

"Mathematics?"

"Yeah. I'd eventually like to work on the space program."

"I can't think of a better place for you."

"Thank you. Studying math is something I've always wanted to do for quite a while."

"That long, huh?"

"My mother will freak."

"You don't think she'll approve?"

"She's the one who talked me into dental hygiene. She thinks I'm flighty. But it's my life. I mean, I have to follow my own calling. I was thinking about it the other night, and I said to myself, 'If I were you–'"

"But you appeared to love the idea of a career as a dental hygienist. You talked about how exciting it would be to console people undergoing root canals, traveling to underdeveloped countries to give flossing seminars–"

"I can't stand the school. I decided I had to get out. So now I have to meet my mother to tell her. I'll just explain to her that the main reason I'm going into math is that I like to finish what I start."

"I don't see how she could argue with that. Anyway, getting back to the reason that you're here–did you ever read *Good Health Is All in Your Mind* like I suggested?"

"Well, no, but a long time ago, I read some xeroxed pages from it."

"Chardonnay, I don't cure your headaches. I just give you information on how to cure yourself. I help you establish a pain-management program. But you have to do all the work."

"It's helping, our sessions."

"I don't see how. You never do anything I suggest."

"No, you're great."

"This is our fourteenth session. Usually I only have six or seven per client, along with periodic follow-up sessions."

"I guess I'm kind of a tough nut to crack."

"*Nut* is the operative word."

$\mathscr{F}$IFTEEN

Dutchman called to say he had been admitted to the hospital for a day or two. He asked Applegate to stop by his apartment and pick up a few things to bring to him. Calvin was in Michigan visiting his aunt.

Applegate let himself into the apartment with his key; most friends-in-need kept keys to their clients' apartments for just such circumstances as these. There was a light on in the dining room.

"Oh, hi, Ogden."

Ogden was sitting at the table, sorting through papers. He looked up and said, "Hi, Applegate."

"I've come by for a few of Dutchman's things. Did you know he's in the hospital?"

"Yes, he called me after he spoke to you. He wanted me to meet you here to give him some papers he needs."

"I told him I should hold onto his medical papers, but he said he preferred to keep them here."

Applegate gathered up the things Dutchman had requested. When he got back to the dining room, Ogden was intently reading a document. Ogden asked, "Didn't you and Dutchman make out his will?"

"Yes, we worked on it. I sent it to the lawyer who takes care of legal matters for the clinic, and then I notarized Dutchman's signature."

"Look at this."

Ogden handed Applegate a crudely drawn up will, signed by Dutchman, in which Dutchman left everything to Calvin.

Applegate was perplexed. "Dutchman never mentioned this will."

"According to the date, this was drawn up right around the time he had his last attack of PCP, which is just before you started seeing him. I'll never forget it. I was the one who found him and got him to the hospital. I had been calling him all day and he didn't answer, which was strange since we had talked about going shopping together. I came over that night and let myself in with my key. There was Dutchman, unconscious on the floor. We figured out later that he had been there at least 10 hours, drifting in and out of consciousness, barely able to breathe."

Applegate shivered at the image. "It must have been terrifying for him, to be that helpless and all alone."

Ogden looked intently at Applegate. "He wasn't alone."

"What do you mean?"

"When I walked in and found Dutchman, Calvin was there. He said he'd just gotten in a minute earlier."

"Dutchman told me you found him, but he never said Calvin had been there. What was Calvin doing? Kneeling by him?"

"He was in the kitchen."

"Dutchman doesn't have a phone in the kitchen."

"He said he went to get him a glass of water."

"Why?"

"He said he panicked. But you know what?"

"What?"

"As the paramedics were taking Dutchman out, I went into the dining room to get his medicine, and I glanced in the kitchen, and there were cookies and milk on the table."

Applegate asked in a stupor, "Cookies and milk?"

"With Dutchman lying there, Calvin had been eating cookies and milk. He wasn't expecting anyone to walk in on him like I did. He'd been sitting there, eating cookies and milk. With Dutchman on the floor, barely alive."

"Does Dutchman know?"

"I'm not sure. He was pretty far gone. He might not have seen Calvin come in. I don't know. But I don't think he knows about this bogus will."

Applegate indicated the papers on the table. "Is the real will here?"

"I couldn't find it."

He studied the will Ogden had found. "This looks like Dutchman's signature."

"Calvin might have had him sign it when Dutchman was on medication."

"But all Dutchman has in the world is a few hundred dollars he got in his grandpa's will. Would Calvin actually let him die for that little money?"

$\mathscr{S}$IXTEEN

Across town at the Blue Gardenia, Pinkerton asked Calvin, "Your floating aunt in Michigan, huh?"

Calvin looked at Pinkerton and asked, "What do you mean?"

"You told Dutchman your Aunt Ruby in Lewiston was sick again?"

"Yeah?"

"Last time Dutchman got sick, you told him Aunt Ruby lived in Chesaning."

"Oh my God! Did I?"

"Yep."

Calvin rolled his shoulders smugly. "Well, Dutchman didn't seem to notice."

"People with PCP pneumonia don't pay a lot of attention to details."

"Look, I love Dutchman. Not like I love you–I'm in love with you."

Pinkerton grunted, "That's a treat!"

Calvin continued, "But I love him like a brother."

Pinkerton thought to himself, "Like Cain loved Abel," and said aloud, "you won't visit him in the hospital?"

"I don't go anywhere near hospitals. I can't stand them." He took Pinkerton's hand and sighed, "Just think, when Dutchman dies, we'll be together every day–"

"Look–"

"–even if it's when I visit you in prison."

"Prison?"

Calvin took a nonchalant sip of his martini. "You know, like if the cops should hear a certain rumor about that hustler who was found dead under the el tracks…"

"That was an accident."

Calvin put his hand to his heart. "I believe you. But will the cops?"

"What are you saying?"

"Just that when I love a man like I love you, he never leaves me. Get used to it. I'm yours for life."

Throckmorton walked up behind them and said, "You're here a little early, aren't you?"

Pinkerton turned around. "Hi, Throckmorton."

Throckmorton was temporarily flustered. "Oh, Pinkerton! It's you! From behind I thought you were… never mind. How are you?"

"Great. And this is my friend, Calvin."

Throckmorton extended a hand and said, "Enchanted."

$\mathscr{S}$EVENTEEN

Matt was putting some books on the shelves when he heard someone enter the store. He turned around to see a beautiful young lady with long black hair.

"Good afternoon. May I help you?"

"Hi, I'm Chardonnay."

"Hi, Chardonnay. I'm Matthew. I'm pleased to meet you."

"Do you like these earrings?"

"Let me see." He walked over to examine them closely while Chardonnay held her hair back. "Yes, very nice."

"Just very nice?"

"Actually, they're quite spectacular."

She smiled. "Really? Spectacular?"

"Yes."

"I get a lot of compliments on them."

Matthew thought to himself, "Gee, I wonder why!" He asked her, "Were you looking for a book?"

"Yeah, do you have *Good Health Is All in Your Mind?*"

"As a matter of fact, I do. It's one of my personal favorites."

"Really? Is it good?"

"Excellent. It gave me a lot of insight into my migraine problem."

Chardonnay was excited. "No kidding? Migraines? That's why I'm reading it. Jerry Applegate recommended it."

"Who's he?"

She asked incredulously, "Who's Jerry Applegate? You get migraines, and you don't know Jerry Applegate? He's just the foremost expert on migraines in the country."

"Does he practice around here?"

"A few blocks away. I'll give you his card."

She handed Matthew Applegate's business card. "Give him a call. He's fantastic."

"Maybe I will."

After paying for the book, Chardonnay looked around and said, "God, this place is so cool. What kind of coffee is that I smell?"

"Today I'm making hazelnut. Would you like a cup?"

"Sure, thanks."

Matthew brought her a cup and indicated the easy chair for her. She asked, "What's that you're reading?"

"Oh, a mediocre novel. It brings back a lot of memories."

"Why?"

"Well, the protagonist is talking about growing up Catholic. He was an altar boy. Do you know what *Dominus vobiscum* means?"

Chardonnay was suddenly angry. She snapped at Matthew, "What's that? Latin? Is that supposed to impress me?"

Matt was surprised by her anger. He fumbled with his words. "Well... it's from the old Latin mass." She glared at him. He tried to explain, "See, they used to have mass in Latin–"

She interrupted him, "I'm not stupid!"

Matt again was confused. "No, I didn't mean–"

"I know they used to have mass in Latin. So what?" It was more of a challenge than a question.

"Well, it's just that, when I read that in the novel, that *Domin–*" Matt stopped, fearing that the phrase might anger Chardonnay again. "When I read that about the Latin mass, it brought back a flood of good memories of being an altar boy and growing up with nuns and confession and stations of the cross." Chardonnay, still angry, merely stared at him. "See, if you're Catholic–"

"I am! That's why I'm so angry."

"Why? What did they do to you?"

Chardonnay exploded, "No, at you! Acting like I don't know about Latin mass. I mean, I'm Italian, aren't I?"

"I'm sorry, I didn't know you were Italian."

"What's wrong with Italians?"

Matthew could only grunt, "Huh?"

"And about 100 percent of Italians are Catholic." She pouted a moment and then asked, "Do you like this necklace?"

Matt felt like he was sinking in quicksand. Lacking anything better to say, he told her, "Yes, the necklace is very nice. What is it, jade?"

"Does it go with my eyes?"

"Well, sure–"

"It's just that you came on so condescending. I know what *Dominus vobiscum* means! Christ! I went to mass often enough as a kid."

"Well, then, I thought maybe it would bring back some nice memories."

"Why did you think it would bring back memories for me if you didn't know I was Catholic?"

"I don't– I mean, I just thought that if–"

She waved at him with one hand, rose and said, "I can't talk to you when you're like this."

"You just met me."

Now she was excited and sparkling as she said, "So if I can pick up on your moods already, I guess I must know you pretty well, huh?"

"You know me?"

"I can spot right away when you're being condescending."

"But I don't think I was–"

"And when you're blocking. You're heavily into denial right now."

"No I'm not… I mean… I mean…"

"I've gotta go. I'll come back in a few days to discuss your problem further." With that she took her book and skipped out the door, calling back, *"Dominus vobiscum!"* ("May the Lord be with you.")

Matt, standing in the doorway, automatically muttered the response he had chanted hundreds of times as a boy, *"Et cum spiritu tuo"* ("And with your spirit.")

That evening, Matthew was sitting at the bar in the Blue Gardenia. He called the bartender over.

"Howie, I've got a problem. I can't pay my tab tonight."

"That's okay. There's no rush."

"I mean someone swiped my wallet."

Howie smacked his hand on the bar and yelled, "God damn it!"

"I'm sorry, but I–"

"Not you! Pinkerton!"

"Pinkerton?"

"He was in here all afternoon, left just about an hour after you showed up. I should have thrown him out. Slimy pickpocket! We've had trouble with him before."

"You think he's the one–"

"I'm sure of it. You know him?"

"I've seen him from a distance."

"One night, he picked up this kid. The kid was too young to even be in here, but it was below zero out and he had no place to stay, and I felt sorry for him. So the kid leaves with Pinkerton. Next thing I hear, the kid's in the hospital. But he wouldn't tell me what happened. Then he disappeared, like hustlers always do."

"I can't stand anyone who mistreats a hustler."

"This guy is such an asshole."

"Throckmorton once told me Pinkerton and I look alike."

Howie squinted at Matthew a moment. "Well, maybe if I was real drunk, and the lights were low…"

"That's just great."

"Tell you what, forget about tonight's tab. It's on the house. Take it as my apology for not throwing that asshole out when I first saw him."

"Thanks. But it wasn't the money that's the big loss. There's this business card, some migraine guy I was going to call."

$\mathcal{E}$IGHTEEN

Having a few beers at Sidetrack on a Wednesday evening, Applegate noticed an attractive stranger sitting alone at the bar and watching the videos. The stools to either side of him were occupied. Applegate glanced over every few minutes, but the stranger appeared not to notice him.

Wednesday was "Showtunes" night at Sidetrack, a large video bar on Halsted. Marilyn Monroe and Jane Russell had just finished singing "Just Two Little Girls from Little Rock", and now Judy Garland was performing her rendition of "My Kind of Town." Earlier, Applegate had been treated to the dubious pleasure of hearing Dolly Parton interpret from *Best Little Whorehouse in Texas*. The surprise of the evening was a clip from *I Love Lucy* with guest-star Tallulah Bankhead.

When a man sitting next to the stranger left, Applegate walked over and took the vacant stool. The stranger glanced at him a moment. Their eyes met. He nodded slightly at Applegate. There was a subtle spark in the stranger's eyes. Applegate nodded back. The stranger turned to the videos. Applegate thought he discerned a knowing, almost smug expression on his face.

After a few moments, the stranger looked away from the screen. Applegate asked, "Do you know a lot of movies?"

The man smiled. "Quite a few."

"See, I've got this line in my head, and I don't know where it's from. It's been driving me crazy trying to figure out where I heard it."

"What's the line?"

"Someone is shouting, 'If I say it's safe to surf this beach, it's safe to surf this beach.'"

The man took a sip of his beer and said, "It's from *Apocalypse Now*. Robert Duval says it. In the same scene he says, 'I love the smell of napalm in the morning.'"

"Okay, I remember. Geez, I was thinking it was from a Beach Blanket movie… that Frankie said it to Annette."

"Hardly. Do you know musicals?"

"A lot of them." Applegate smiled. It was working. The stranger was responding. Then Applegate realized he had forgotten to ask his name. Well, it was too late now. He'd have to wait for an appropriate moment.

The stranger asked, "Okay, what musical is this line from: 'Your eyes are the eyes of a woman in love, and, oh, how they give you away.'"

"I know I know it…"

"Do you want a clue?"

"Yeah."

"Here's the clue: 'Please, please don't shoot me just because I beat up your sister.'"

"I know that too. From the newspapers. That actor's son… He shot his sister's husband. There was a trial."

"So who's the actor?"

Applegate got excited. "He was in *Apocalypse Now*."

"Very good. What's his name?"

"Wait. Marlon Brando."

"Right."

Applegate was confused. "Marlon Brando sang that?"

"Yes."

"In *Apocalypse Now*?"

The stranger laughed. "No, Brando sang it in another movie."

Now Applegate remembered. "Oh, right. As Sky Masterson in *Guys and Dolls.*"

The stranger asked, "How about this: 'Sodomy, fellatio, cunnilingus, pederasty. Father, why do these words sound so nasty?'"

"I know that. *Hair*."

"Right."

Applegate said, "Now let me try. 'When you were trembling on the brink, was I out somewhere winking at a star?'"

"Oh! Oh! I know it!"

"Well?"

"He's singing it in front of a fountain outdoors…"

"Right."

"But I can't think of the name."

"Want a clue?"

"Yeah."

Applegate smiled. "I'll give you one as helpful as the one you gave me. Here goes." Applegate said, very quickly with no pauses, "'What do you talk? What do you talk? What do you talk? What do you talk?'"

"That's from *The Music Man*."

"Right."

"And that's a clue?"

"Yep."

The stranger said, "Oh, the line is from *Gigi*."

"Yeah."

"So what's that got to do with *The Music Man*?"

"Hermione Gingold was in both movies."

"Hmmm. Good clue." He extended his hand and said, "My name is Kevin."

"Hi, I'm Applegate."

They held the handshake for several moments longer than necessary. Kevin's expression was knowing and erotic.

Kevin said, "I don't often get to have a night out unsupervised. The old biddy keeps me on a short leash."

"Sounds like you live with Nancy Reagan."

"Worse. And his name is Alex."

"Your lover?"

"Hell no. Just a roommate. But very neurotic. He's at a tupperware party with his girlfriends tonight."

"Honest to God? An actual tupperware party?"

"Yeah, he goes in for that kind of B.S. He's sulking because we had this tremendous fight the other day."

"What about?"

"I don't know; he never told me."

"Does Alex like musicals?"

"His idea of a musical is watching some heavy metal morons smash their instruments." He sipped his beer with a sly, knowing look and said, "I have a recording of Helen Humes singing from *Porgy and Bess*."

Applegate snapped at the bait. "No kidding!"

"You can't believe how she delivers 'The Strawberry Woman'."

"The best I've heard do that is Ella Fitzgerald."

"Ella does it great, but Helen... You know how she sounds like a little kid, and then she tries for a high note, and you think she won't be able to reach it? And then–"

"Right, and then she just leaps over it effortlessly!"

Kevin closed his eyes and smacked his lips. "Plus I have the original cast of *Sweet Charity*. With Gwen Verdon. Not Shirley MacLaine."

"I didn't care for Shirley in the movie."

"You'll love Gwen."

"Yeah, one of my favorites. I'll never forget her locker room dance in *Damn Yankees*."

"Did you know she was married to Bob Fosse?"

"Did I know? I've been jealous since I found out."

"So, want to hear it?"

"You mean tonight?"

"Sure, we'd have the place to ourselves."

"Look, Kevin, you're a nice guy, and I like you a lot..."

"So?"

"And I'd love to go to your place..."

"But?"

"I have a lot of problems. I think you need to know... well, that I can't... I mean..."

"Come on, we're both men of the world."

"No I'm not."

"Neither am I. But why do you assume I'm trying to make you? Don't you think gay men can have a friendship without sex?"

Now Applegate felt naive. "I didn't mean that..."

Kevin placed a reassuring hand on Applegate's shoulder. "Look, just come up to my place, we'll hear some music, no strings attached." When Applegate hesitated Kevin said, "Maybe I don't even find you attractive, did you ever consider that? Maybe I'm just happy to find someone who shares my taste in music."

Applegate smiled and said, "Kevin, I'm sorry."

"Forget it. Ready?"

Applegate finished his beer, smacked the glass on the bar and said, "Let's go!"

When they walked into Kevin's apartment, the first thing Kevin said was, "Let's get nekkid!" He began to unbutton his shirt.

Applegate shouted, "What? No! Wait! Wait!" Kevin looked at him innocently. Applegate said, "Let me do that for you." He walked over and unbuttoned the remaining buttons. He removed Kevin's shirt and caressed his bare chest.

Kevin said, "Your turn!"

Applegate turned away and walked to the stereo. "No, not yet. Let's hear that Gwen Verdon."

Kevin started the tape and went into the kitchen. He returned with two glasses of white wine and a bowl of fruit. He handed one glass to Applegate and placed the fruit on the coffee table.

"Help yourself. I thought you might like a snack." Kevin picked up a banana. He held it in his hand casually as they spoke. "I haven't seen you around before."

"Tonight was only my third time in Sidetrack. I'm kind of new to the gay scene."

Kevin thought to himself, "I can tell by that outfit," but said aloud, "just coming out? At... what? Twenty-five years old?"

"Thank you. Twenty-nine."

"A beautiful age. Trembling on the brink."

Applegate smiled. "You make me sound like Gigi."

Kevin was stroking the banana up and down with his thumb and two middle fingers. He fluttered his fingers ever so slightly. When he came to the end, he subtly tickled it under the stem.

Kevin said, "Sidetrack is a nice place."

His index finger was still under the stem of the banana, now rubbing it slowly. He moved his hand up around the end, until the tip was nestled inside his cupped palm. He squeezed gently.

Kevin continued, "If you want to get an overview of the nightlife, check out the Halsted Street Fair in August. It's like Chicago's Mardi Gras. All the gay bars along the Halsted strip open up onto the street. It gets pretty wild."

Kevin began to peel the banana. He bent back on the tip and slowly, obscenely, pulled it away to reveal the white flesh. In the background, Gwen Verdon and company were asking whether Applegate wanted to have a [BOOM BOOM] good time.

The sight of the white, exposed banana flesh worked to break down any barriers between the two men. Applegate felt as though Kevin were already inside him. Kevin playfully poked it into his mouth, but withdrew it with only a lick. Holding it near his lower lip, he said, "The Blue Gardenia is real nice. Quiet, informal." He nonchalantly rolled his tongue around the tip, all the while staring into Applegate's eyes.

Applegate said, "Yeah, Blue... Blue Gardenia. Informal banana..."

Kevin licked the banana, all the way from base to tip, with his full tongue. "Right, you've got it. Informal banana. That's what it's all about."

He held the banana out to Applegate. "Here, have a taste."

Applegate was having difficulty responding verbally. He put his lips to the fruit.

Kevin said, "Go ahead, give me a lick. I can't wait to have you lick it." Applegate opened his mouth and extended his tongue. Kevin impulsively withdrew the banana.

"On second thought, that's enough of that." He replaced the peel and set the opened banana back in the bowl of fruit. "I know you must love Billie Holiday."

"Yeah, Billie."

Kevin crossed the room to the stereo and changed the tape. The lazy, narcotic, cracked-china voice of Lady Day began singing of how Kevin's lips were the doors to ecstasy.

Kevin picked up a strawberry. He took a bite, then held it out to Applegate. Applegate retreated slightly, lying back onto the couch, his head resting on the arm. Now the strawberry was suspended over his mouth. A drop of red juice dripped onto his face, above his upper lip. The aroma of strawberry was sudden and wonderful, evoking images of green leaves and tender vines. Applegate's tongue darted out at the drop just under his nose, and the taste of strawberry intensified the aroma.

Applegate reached out to touch Kevin's trousers. They were light and cottony, smooth and soft. He placed a finger under the waistline, caught the elastic of Kevin's shorts, and gave it a snap. The sound amused him; he snapped the waistband again. They both laughed. Kevin brought the strawberry down onto Applegate's mouth, rubbing it over his lips. Applegate nodded slightly, then took a bite.

Kevin sat back and grabbed a peach, one that was slightly brown and off-pitch. Like a little boy, he unceremoniously took a huge bite. The peach, somewhat overripe, gushed into his mouth and around his lips. He slurped the flesh and licked the prodigious juices from around his mouth. Drops of thick, sweet peach nectar glistened down his chin. He used both hands to smear the nectar into his bare chest. The hair on his nipples glistened. He dipped a finger in his wine and brought it to Applegate's mouth. Applegate leapt forward, instinctively wrapping his lips around it.

Kevin smiled. "Now it's your turn." He reached out with both hands and began to unbutton Applegate's shirt.

Applegate writhed against Kevin's small, precise fingers. Kevin's hands worked their way down Applegate's chest to his belly. Applegate was hypnotized by the gentle rhythm of Kevin's breathing, by its warmth on his cheeks. His mouth retained subtle traces of wine and sweet peach nectar. He noticed some drops still glistening on Kevin's chin. He leaned forward and licked them off.

Kevin glided his fingertips over Applegate's forehead and cheeks, behind his ears, across the back of his neck. Applegate's shirt appeared to float off his body of its own accord. Kevin ran his moist fingers up and down Applegate's bare torso, pausing at his nipples and navel, detouring under Applegate's arms and down his sides.

Applegate lay back on the couch, arching his pelvis upward. Kevin covered him with his own body, supporting himself on one arm, unbuckling Applegate's belt with his free hand, kissing Applegate on the mouth.

Kevin's tongue darted against Applegate's, his hand now unzipping Applegate's jeans. Suddenly Applegate was overwhelmed with confusion. He looked at Kevin and felt a surge of terror as he saw his father's face looking down at him. The face was evil and distorted in rage. The room suddenly appeared filthy; there was a smell of excrement. Something slimy was crawling on Applegate's body. He thought he saw cockroaches swarming over the couch.

Before he could respond, the face above him changed again, this time to Dr. Bellman. Now Applegate felt a rush of raw, sexual passion. The universe was clean. No, not just clean. The phrase he thought of, that kept running through his mind, was spic-n-span. He winced at the ridiculousness of the words, but he kept thinking, "The universe is spic-n-span."

For one brief moment, horror battled with intimacy; then Applegate saw Kevin emerge from the fog. There was no filth. There was no god-like Adonis. Kevin was a human being, here with him now, warm and refreshing, new and alluring. Utterly new and real.

Between kisses Kevin was asking him, "So, are you a top or a bottom?"

"I'm… I'm flexible."

Kevin maneuvered Applegate face-down on the couch, a large, plump pillow beneath his hips. His rear end stuck up as Kevin kissed and caressed.

A tube of lubricant appeared from nowhere. Kevin squeezed some onto his finger and smeared it around. At what he thought was the right moment, Kevin inserted his finger.

"YEEEEEOOOOOWWWWW!!!!!!!" Applegate nearly fell to the floor. "What did you do to me?"

Kevin looked at him. "What? What happened?"

"That hurt!" Applegate rubbed himself and continued, "You got a hangnail?"

"No, I keep 'em trimmed. Look." He held out his hand for Applegate to examine.

"Then what happened?"

"Let me check. Come on, get back in position. I promise I won't hurt you. That's it. Get your butt up a little more." Applegate, bent over the pillow, stuck his rump as high into the air as he could. Kevin peered deeply and asked, "Baby, don't you know you've got piles?"

Applegate raised himself to a kneeling position, looked back over his shoulder at Kevin and asked, "What?! Piles? What's that?"

Kevin gently pressed Applegate's head back down and said, "You don't know what are piles? Hemorrhoids."

"I don't have hemorrhoids!"

"Lambie-pie, take it from me. I'm practically a proctologist. You have an external hemorrhoid. Didn't you ever notice it?"

"Well, maybe…"

"Ain't no maybe about it. Doesn't it ever bother you?"

"Sometimes there's some discomfort."

Kevin affirmed, "They come and go."

"But I have a little dildo I practice with! I like my dildo—"

"Sure, when they're not swollen. Honey, piles is a come-and-go thing. When they're down, yeah, you can fuck your brains out. But they're here tonight." He continued to hold Applegate's cheeks spread wide, examining the troubled spot.

"How can I have hemorrhoids? I work out!"

"I can see you do. Nice shoulder development, muscular legs. I bet you swim a lot."

"Three times a week."

"What are you, about 170 pounds?"

"Bingo. So how can I—"

"It's got nothing to do with exercise. Lots of athletes get them. Hemorrhoids are caused by walking on two legs. The amazing thing is that we don't all have them."

"But I don't want to have piles!"

"I think that goes without saying. Let me try finger-fucking you again. I have an idea."

"Well, if you're real careful."

"First I'll apply a little lube right to the hemorrhoid itself..."

Kevin squeezed the lubricant onto the afflicted area. "How's that?"

Applegate sighed deeply and purred, "Wonderful."

"Good. I'll spread it around, very gentle... "

"Yeah, that's right... Yeah..."

"Now I'll try just a little penetration—"

"YEEEEEEOOOOOOOWWWWWWWW!!!!!!!"

"Well, enough of that."

Suddenly there was a tremendous pounding at the door.

"Damn you Kevin! You have a man in there, don't you!!! I'll kill you both this time! Kevin! I have a gun!" The pounding became frantic.

Kevin, wearing only his pants, jumped up. "Ohmygod! It's Alex! You have to hide!"

"I hear you in there! I'll kill you, you lying little tramp!"

"Quick, into the bathtub."

Applegate, naked and dazed, muttered, "The bathtub?"

Kevin grabbed Applegate's clothes, shoved them into his arms and pulled him along, frantically whispering, "He'll never think to look in there. Leave the door open, hide behind the shower curtain. He'll just glance in the bathroom. He won't see anything, and I'll get rid of him."

"I don't—" but Kevin shoved him towards the tub and turned to the hallway.

"Coming, darling."

Applegate stood in the tub behind the shower curtain and listened. He heard the door open. It sounded as though Alex practically fell into the apartment.

"Sweetheart! You're home early! What a lovely surprise!"

"Why was the door bolted? Where is he?" He looked at the coffeetable. "The strawberry and wine routine? He must have been a real moron to fall for that old shtick."

"What do you mean? I'm all alone. Do you want a drink?"

Applegate's hand was touching the shower curtain. He felt a weird sensation on his thumb but ignored it as he listened to the two men in the hallway.

"I'll bet he's in the bathtub, isn't he? That's where you hide all your cheap–"

"Alexander, my love, my little love, I swear to you I'm all alone. Don't you trust me?"

The voices approached the bathroom. Applegate tensed up and failed to pay attention to the weird sensation which was now making its way up his arm.

Kevin sounded very firm, "Alexander, this has gone too far."

"Get out of my way!" They were just outside the bathroom door.

Kevin's voice approached a shriek, "I mean it, Alex. These jealous rages have to STOP! NOW! I'm all alone. You have to learn to trust me or we're through. Do you understand? If you go searching this apartment, I'm… I'm moving out."

Alex's voice quavered with fear as he said, "You don't mean that."

"Don't push me, baby. I'm always faithful to you. I try. God knows how I… how I…" His voice began to tremble slightly. Applegate was fascinated–he found himself believing that Kevin was faithful to Alex.

"Kevin! Do you mean it? Kevin, don't cry."

Now Kevin's voice rose and the tremble mushroomed into a sob. "You don't believe a word I say! You don't love me!"

"Oh, baby, of course I–"

Alex must have tried to embrace Kevin, because Applegate could hear Kevin push him against the same wall that separated them from him.

"You don't! You don't love me! Or you would trust me!"

"I do, I do trust you–"

"Then what are you storming in here for please? Answer me that I'm sure!"

The two men were so close Applegate could hear Alex's quick, shallow breaths. "Please, honey, I'm sorry. I'll never do it again, I swear. I'm so sorry. It's just that I love you so damn much. The thought of you and another man…"

Applegate could hear the gentle crinkle of Alex's shirt against Kevin's bare chest. He heard soft caresses and tiny kisses.

Kevin purred, "Let's go out for ice cream. You know what jamoca almond fudge does to me."

Alex was entranced. "Sure. Anything."

Kevin suddenly shouted, "Where are you going?"

"I'll be right back. I just have to take a leak–"

"No! You're checking up on me!"

"Oh for God's sake! I'll go at Baskin-Robbins."

Applegate silently sighed as he heard their footsteps go down the hallway. Now the weird sensation was on his bare shoulder. He turned to look.

He found himself eyeball-to-eyeball with a cockroach. The creature was nonchalantly sitting on his shoulder, apparently preparing to frolic through Applegate's hair.

There was a moment of peace and wonder as the two beings contemplated each other, a brief interval of calm preceding the mindless, barbaric panic about to ensue. Applegate looked at the newcomer with the same expression he would give a man on the street who seemed familiar, but whose name he had forgotten.

Just as they were locking the door behind them, Kevin and Alex heard a thunderous crash and savage shrieking.

Alex asked, "What's that?"

"Nothing. That's the neighbor girl and her little friends."

"No it isn't! That's coming from our place!"

"No! You don't trust me!"

"Shut up!" Alex shoved Kevin aside and ran through the apartment. Applegate's screaming was unabated for the several moments that he struggled on the bathroom floor, entangled in the shower curtain and the soap-on-a-rope which was nearly strangling him. As soon as he managed to get free, he lunged at the bathroom door. Unfortunately, Alex was at that moment on the other side reaching for the knob and was struck violently in the forehead.

Alex held his head and shrieked, "He tried to kill me! Your little whore tried to kill me!"

Kevin comforted Alex. Alex shouted, "I'm bleeding! I'm bleeding! Is this what you want? You want me dead?"

Applegate stood in the doorway, naked, stunned and shivering with fear. He tried to explain, "The big... black..."

Alex shrieked, "You've got Tyrone in there too! Kevin, how could you? Cheating on me with two at a time! Making a sandwich!? With you in the middle!?"

"Babycakes, Tyrone is history. I would never–" Kevin noticed that Applegate was merely standing in the doorway, watching like it was the latest episode of *All My Children*. He bared his teeth and hissed, "Leave stupid!"

Applegate gathered his clothes and maundered off, saying to no one in particular, "The big... black... that face..." He wandered down the hallway, then out the door. Closing it behind him, he began to dress on the stairway.

Kevin was on his knees. "I swear he followed me home and FORCED his way in. Said he wanted to call a cab. Once I let him in, he said he had to use the bathroom. The next thing I know, you came. I didn't know he was naked in there! God knows what he was planning to do to me!"

"You expect me to believe–"

Now Kevin was pouty and self-pitying. "And I couldn't tell you he was there, because I knew you'd think the worst of me! You always convict me; you never give me the preponderance of the evidence! You jump at the slightest incrimination! I couldn't trust you to believe me!"

Alex sounded very unsure as he began, "Well, you must admit it looks–"

"LOOKS! LOOKS! What does looks mean? Joan of Arc looked guilty, but she was a saint! They almost burned her at the stake on circumstantial evidence. If the Sheriff of Nottingham hadn't pardoned her at the last minute, she would have died! Died!"

Alex's grasp of history was even more tenuous than Kevin's. "The Sheriff of Nottingham?"

Kevin's face was red as he continued, "What about our love? Isn't that real? You say you love me, but you don't believe me! The only reason that pervert was in the bathtub in the first place is because I knew I couldn't turn to you without you blaming me! I can't count on you to be there when I need help!"

"Baby, please, calm down. I can't stand to see you like this." Alex tried to embrace him.

Kevin pushed him away, yelling, "No, go back to your tupperware party! Go ahead! I'll go after the pervert and tell him it's okay with you if he rapes and kills me! Go ahead!"

"Kevin, I–"

"If you can't trust me, if my feelings for you mean noth… noth… nothing…" He trailed off into tears.

Alex took him in his arms and caressed him. "I've been a fool. Of course I believe you, baby. You're too gullible for your own good. You should have known he was a liar. Nobody phones for a cab in this part of the city."

Kevin looked anxiously over his shoulder, shivered in terror at what might have befallen him, and then buried his face in Alex's chest. In his best *That Girl* voice he rasped, "Thank God you got here when you did."

Alex comforted him. "It's okay, baby. A sweet little dish like you, God knows he might have tried. Do you know his name?"

"He said it was Lloyd, but I didn't believe him."

"Yeah, honesty don't mean shit to his type. You want I should go after him and rough him up?"

Kevin pondered a minute. The image of two men fighting over him was tempting… but he looked at Alex's 145 pounds, and thought of Applegate's 170 pounds and muscular frame. "No, leave the poor degenerate alone. I wouldn't want you to get your hands dirty. You might get carried away and kill him. His punishment is just being who he is."

INETEEN

Matthew was thinking that this would be a perfect time to smoke a ciga-rette… if he smoked. It was about 1:00 a.m. Duke had fallen asleep next to him. He'd only been asleep a few minutes, and Matt knew he must wake him. Duke would be upset if Matt let him sleep through the most profitable part of his work week. But Matt couldn't resist the temptation to sit back and stare at Duke for a few minutes.

Duke was typical of the hustlers Matt encountered along Belmont on a late Saturday night: bluejeans and a white T-shirt, cigarettes rolled up in the sleeve, baseball cap, tennis shoes. Tough look contrasted by sad and hungry eyes. They always tried so hard to look fearless and worldly, but the eyes inex-orably gave them away. And when they fell asleep–a rarity on Saturday night, since they could still make more money, but a common occurrence on week-nights when what they wanted even more than the forty dollars was a place to stay–they looked angelic. They could pose along Belmont, but once they fell asleep, they relaxed into what they really were.

What was this one's name? Oh yes, "Duke". Matt would guess he was twen-ty years old, but that was when Duke was leaning against a building in the dark, smoking a cigarette and sneering. Now that he was asleep, he looked more like fourteen. Matt was always telling his friends that he wanted a man, not a boy. Yet here he was once again with a young hustler.

It was only two or three years ago that Matt's obsession with hustlers had begun. He had seen them many times along Halsted or down Belmont, sometimes alone, sometimes a group of them looking like a pride of stray cats. Their voices, when they would call to him, would curl around him like a feline rubbing around his legs. He generally ignored them. He didn't fully understand how they fit into gay life at all, much less into his life.

But that night, years ago, as he was walking home leisurely well after midnight, one particular hustler had caught his eye. The kid looked about fifteen. He was standing in the proper hustler stance. He was wearing the correct clothes, and yet he didn't fit in. The arrogance was more studied than in most. There was a slight shudder in his face when his eyes met Matt's.

And what eyes they were! Large, green, cat-like! They startled Matt. It was as if Matt were seeing the world for the first time, as if a veil were lifted which had prevented Matt from understanding the plight of these young men.

The child was obviously frightened. Matt walked towards him; he walked slowly, making no sudden moves. The child stiffened at his approach. Yet he paradoxically leaned back slightly, striking an unmistakably sexual pose.

There was something going through Matt's mind as he walked up to the young man. It was music. Matt could almost hear chords being played on a guitar. Then it struck him: he was being reminded of that autumn afternoon, over a decade ago, when he and Roger had gone off to the woods. Something about the green eyes of this child was making that afternoon live again; something in the terrified face and arrogant mouth was making the music present for Matt.

Matt felt a bond with the young man before him. The few stray chords from that russet afternoon compelled him to try to make contact.

"Hi. My name is Matt."

"I'm Rick. How's it hanging, man?"

The kid didn't understand. Matt asked, "Are you okay? Are you hungry?"

The child's eyes took on a glimmer of defiance. He smiled and asked, "Looking for some action? Feeling hot?"

They were talking past each other. Matt was disoriented in the same dreamlike euphoria which a particularly moving novel can bring on. He was feeling that Rick was somehow important to him.

Rick interpreted Matt's concern as a challenge he must repulse. Matt asked, "Can we talk somewhere? Like over coffee?"

"What are you fucking around for? Are you buying or not?"

"What I want... see, I can help you."

"I don't need any help. I'm just fine."

"No you're not. You're too young–"

"I'm eighteen."

"No you're not."

"You calling me a liar, asshole?"

"Hey, I'm just trying–"

But the more Matt attempted to reach Rick, the more determined Rick was to remain separate. Rick had walked away cursing.

After that fledgling attempt, Matt felt a desperate need to be with these young men, as if they held some secret knowledge he must discover. He knew that he must play by the rules–their rules–which meant both money and sex.

Matt never actually touched them; they just masturbated together. The sex–if you could call it that–was a hustler's dream: no kissing, no touching, completed in five minutes. It was little more than an excuse to bring them home, wash them up and feed them a good meal. Matt didn't control these young men. They controlled him. They were usually stronger than he was. More than one had beaten and robbed him.

Still, Matt wondered if he was guilty–technically or morally–of some form of child abuse. They were kids. They were underage. It was sex, no matter how he rationalized it. And it was erotic, no matter how sterile he tried to keep it. Matt's knees buckled under him when a young arm would brush against his own as they walked back to his apartment. He trembled when the hustler would bend and arch in the process of removing a T-shirt. His pulse would quicken when a boy's breath caressed his cheek in bed. More than once–after a few beers–Matt had declared love for the vagrant lying next to him.

A deep, sleepy sigh from Duke brought Matthew back to the present. What was it now, sitting in the dark, that so enslaved Matt to this young stranger? The face was beautiful, but to actually kiss it would have been–as he remembered from a movie–"like eating green cantaloupes." Duke's hair–why do they always choose names like "Duke" and "Ace" and "Buddy"?!–was a mass of tight black curls. He was one of the most beautiful boys Matt had ever seen, fit to be a model for Michelangelo.

But it was his smell that hypnotized Matthew. Duke's arm was up over his head, and a sweet, alluring aroma was emanating from his armpit. It was as light as apple blossoms, as intoxicating as lilac leaves before the lavender flowers appear. How did such a boy become so twisted as to sell his body for money? How had Matt come to the lonely pass where he would buy it?

He stared at Duke's closed eyes, inhaled Duke's beguiling aroma, listened to the soft rhythm of Duke's robust, clean breathing. It was getting late. Duke would be angry if Matt let him sleep much longer. Duke could easily make another hundred dollars before dawn.

Matt hesitated. There was a certain excitement at the thought of Duke angry, really angry with him...

Matt reached over and put a hand on Duke's shoulder. Duke mumbled incoherently. Matt shook him gently. Duke's eyes fluttered.

"Hey, Duke, you fell asleep."

"What time is it?"

"About one-thirty."

"How long did I sleep?"

"About twenty minutes."

"I gotta go, man."

Duke rose from the bed. In the light from the few candles around the room, Duke looked much older than he had a minute ago. The candlelight shimmered off the hair of his arms and legs. His calves and thighs were muscular, his penis and pubic hair manly. Only his eyes retained their frightened immaturity.

"Are you sure you have to leave right now? Wouldn't you like to go somewhere for a bite to eat?"

"Are you nuts? I'm having a great night. I'm making money hand over fist."

Matthew thought to himself, "Head over heels," and asked aloud, "when was the last time you had a hot meal?"

Duke looked at Matt insolently and said, "Don't worry about me, grandpa. I do just fine." Matt looked at Duke's arms. He saw track marks.

Matt asked, "How about a sandwich?"

"What do you have?"

"I think I have some baked ham."

Duke was tying his shoelaces. He looked up and asked, "Any Wonder bread?"

"No, but I have rye."

"That's good too. Sure, ham on rye. Do you have mayo?"

"Yeah. I'll be right back."

Matt went into the kitchen and got out the platter of leftover baked ham. He sliced off a few pieces, made a sandwich, and garnished it with mayonnaise and lettuce. He put a pickle slice on the plate and spooned on some potato salad. He brought it all into the bedroom along with a glass of milk.

Duke looked at him and frowned. "No, I meant to-go."

"You want the sandwich to-go?"

Duke smiled an irresistible smile and said, "You don't mind, do you? Just throw it all in a paper sack."

"No, I don't mind. I'll be right back."

Duke got up from the bed and took the plate. "Never mind, I don't need the sack." He grabbed the fork from Matt's hand and took a swift bite of potato salad. He swept up the sandwich and headed for the door. "Good stuff. I'll have to come back when I have more time."

"Sure, I'd like that. Even later tonight if–"

As Duke rushed down the stairs with three twenty-dollar bills in his hand, he called back to Matthew, "Thanks for the tip, grandpa."

WENTY

Applegate leaned forward in his chair and pleaded, "Just give me five more minutes!"

Charles shook his head and whimpered, "You said that ten minutes ago."

"And you got through it. We take it five minutes at a time. I know it hurts, I know you're scared. But we've come this far."

"I don't want to…"

"Look, there's the codeine." Applegate pointed to Charles' prescription bottle on the coffeetable in front of them. "There are enough narcotics in that bottle to knock you on your ass. Any time the pain becomes unbearable, you can take all you want. I'm not going to take them away. I promise."

Charles sat up and reached for the bottle. Applegate shouted, "Wait! Another five minutes! Just go another five minutes!"

Charles was crying. "But then you'll want five more!"

"Don't think about anything but getting through the next five minutes. Don't think about the pain. Concentrate on your breathing. You made it this far, didn't you?"

Charles' hand was hovering over the bottle of codeine. He looked at Applegate. He was terrified. "I don't know."

"What do you mean you don't know? Of course you did."

"Yeah, I did. But you promised–"

"Just five more minutes. Let's try the web in the hand again."

"That doesn't work for me! I want my pills!"

"Concentrate on your breathing. Come on, breathe with me now. Very slowly, inhale. Now exhale. Exhale the pain. Let it go. Release the pain. Now breathe in again."

"You said if I just went five more minutes–"

"Charles, you're here because you want to overcome the migraines."

Charles was very hesitant in his answer. He sensed it was some sort of trap. "I suppose."

"I've asked you to do things for me in the past."

"And I always have! I always followed your instructions! And now I have a migraine again!"

"But I've helped you."

"I have a migraine right now!"

"But I've helped you. You said they were coming less frequently. The massive dose of vitamin B, you said, was the most relief you've ever gotten."

"Yeah, I said that."

"I've helped you. We're making progress. When you've followed my instructions, you've been happy afterwards that you did."

Charles realized he was now in the trap. "Yeah."

"And I promise you, if you listen to me now, you'll be happy you did. I promise this is the most important moment of your life." Charles stared at Applegate. There was fear, but now there was also a glimmer of trust. It was all Applegate needed from him.

Applegate continued, "Okay, sit back and relax. I know you don't believe you can relax, but what we're dealing with here is fear more than pain. If I can help you to relax, the pain will deflate. I've been through it myself. I know what I'm talking about. Now let's try the visualization. Count backwards from ten. We'll do it together." As Applegate went through the count-down, he noticed Charles' hand unclench.

"Concentrate on the tension leaving your body. Visualize the stress starting to escape from your fingers and toes. I want you to look at the migraine. Can you see it?"

Charles concentrated. Finally he said, "Yes, I can see it."

"What color is it?"

"Color?"

"All pain has color and shape. Look at the migraine and describe it for me."

"It's black."

"Very good. The migraine is black. What shape is it?"

"I think it's... It's like an amoeba. It keeps pulsating. It keeps moving..."

"Does it have a face?"

"No, it doesn't have any sort of features. It's like a snake, like a fat, long snake wrapped around my brain, squeezing my head…"

"Listen to me carefully. I'm bigger than the snake. I can kill it. We're going to burn it up. Concentrate on the snake. Take your hands and squeeze the snake. Squeeze it until you've got it all rolled up between your two hands. Have you done that?"

Charles concentrated and finally said, "Yes, I've got the snake all rolled up."

"What's it doing? Is it fighting you?"

"Yes. It's biting at my hands. It has fangs. White fangs in a red mouth."

"It can't hurt you. I'm more powerful than the snake. Now take the snake and bring it to the furnace. Open the furnace door. Do you feel the heat as you open the door?"

"Yes, I feel the heat. I see the flames inside."

"It's a hot furnace. Now throw the snake in. Concentrate on keeping the snake in the furnace as it burns. What color is the smoke?"

"It's purple. Tons and tons of purple smoke."

"Concentrate on the smoke. See the mountains of purple smoke pouring out the chimney. See it go up into the air away from you. Mountains and mountains of purple smoke."

Applegate studied Charles. Charles' head was lying softly against the back of the couch. His shoulders were loose and relaxed. His breathing was regular.

Applegate asked him, "Do you feel any better?"

"Well, a little, maybe. But it still hurts."

Applegate smiled. "Not as much."

Charles sullenly admitted, "No, not quite as much."

"With migraines, we're dealing with fear more than pain. A pain in the head is a terrifying experience; it makes you think of aneurysms and brain tumors. Once I get you through the fear, the pain itself is relatively easy to manage."

"It's one thing to do it in this office. What about when I'm alone? What will I do then?"

"We'll continue our sessions until the tools are your own. I will teach you all the things we do here until you master them." He stared at Charles a moment and said, "I think I should give you a massage now."

Charles reacted a little too quickly, "Our time is almost up."

"I know. But I don't want you to leave just yet."

Charles once again felt trapped; he had been hoping to leave immediately and resort to the codeine as soon as he was out of Applegate's sight. "I can't afford to pay you for a double session."

Applegate read his mind and said, "No charge. And I think it would make you feel a whole lot better."

Charles had no way out (except to tell the truth), and so removed his clothes and got on the massage table, face down.

Applegate put on Japanese folk music, contemplative and soothing. He turned off the overhead light and switched on the peach-shaded lamp in the corner. He began with Charles' shoulders.

Applegate said, "This will be a little different from the massages I've given you in the past. Do you like the music?"

Charles was drained from his session with Applegate. The migraine still hovered in his head but now was manageable. Applegate's movements were wide and light. Charles sounded half-asleep as he responded, "Yes, very nice."

Applegate whispered, "Good."

For the next half hour, Applegate massaged him, shimmering over his skin, touching knots of tension to release them, barely skimming the muscles. Soon Applegate could hear Charles beginning to gently snore.

Applegate pulled a sheet over Charles. He sat down several feet away from the massage table and began to read a book by the light of the single lamp. He looked at Charles and said to himself, "We were lucky this time. If I had let you go, you'd be high as a kite right now. If I hadn't been able to put you to sleep..."

$\mathcal{T}$WENTY-ONE

A Wednesday night at the Blue Gardenia:

"Come on, can't you see it? Bette Davis Beer! It will be a sensation. 'Bette Davis Beer... for the man with a sense of color and fabric.' Or we could have a bunch of construction workers in jeans and hard hats and no shirts with the caption: 'It brings out the Mimsy in you.'"

"So my English professor was saying that class participation would have a bearing effect on our final grade."

"It was the one where Gilligan got hit on the head with a coconut and could read minds."

"The rain forests are being wiped out! Soon there won't be any oxygen! And none of you silly fairies wants to hear it! No one wants to listen to me!"
"I'm sorry, did you say something?"

"You always get to be the submissive one!"

"Matthew! I'm shocked! You? Drinking hard liquor?"
Matthew merely grunted at Throckmorton and poured back a shot of Bom-

bay gin. His body shook a moment, a look of satisfaction crossed his face, and he signalled Howie for another.

Paris said, "Throckmorton, darling, you know what it means when Matt drinks shots."

Throckmorton fluttered his hands dramatically and lamented, "Oh, you have a migraine! Poor dear!"

The bartender poured another shot of Bombay. Matthew saluted Paris and Throckmorton and downed it in a quick gulp. This time he took a few sips of beer for a chaser. He signaled the bartender again.

Paris asked, "Are you sure that's good for you?"

Matthew finally had the wherewithal to speak. "I don't get 'em often, but every few weeks I have a blockbuster. The only thing they respond to is a fifth of gin."

"A fifth? Isn't that a little… extreme?"

"I can deal with a hangover. I can't deal with a migraine." He downed another shot. Now his eyes registered peace and calm as the alcohol worked its numbness throughout his body, easing the stabbing pain in his head and bathing him in a warm aura of goodwill.

"So I told him to be fruitful and multiply. But not in those words."

"It's too soon to take a wait-and-see attitude."

"You have to watch out for Kevin's mood swings."
"Mood swings?! I've only ever seen him in one mood. I wish he did have swings."

"I'm the kind of guy who says I love you and, hey, I mean it."

"How's the painting going?"
"I think I'm on the verge of something big."
"Great."
"I think it's suicide."

"So we were watching Family Feud and the question was 'Name a famous Rudolph.' So Throckmorton says, 'Hitler.'"

Applegate was here tonight also, standing in his usual spot, watching the porno videos, trying to look around the bar, but too intimidated by it all to catch more than a fleeting glance every few minutes.

One of the things Applegate loved about gay bars was that they occasionally introduced him to new jazz vocalists or played some of his favorites. The Blue

Gardenia in particular was noted for devoting an hour or more to singers like Sarah Vaughan or Ella Fitzgerald. Tonight Applegate heard the opening melody of a familiar tune. Billie Holiday was singing about living on pale moonlight, somewhere east of the sun.

As he listened, he happened to catch a slight movement in the distance. He looked into the mirror behind the bar and noticed Matt dreamily mouthing the words along with Lady Day. Applegate was fascinated. He wasn't sure if he recognized him; was this the same man who had asked him what kind of beer he was drinking?

"It was like being up the creek without a paddle."
"It was even worse; it was like being in the pit without the pendulum."

"Well, I'm circumcised, but I met this guy who has a program for re-growing a foreskin."

"Two Jews and a priest walk into a bar…"

"You look ravishing tonight!"
"Yeah, I'm pretty hungry."

"I don't know; do you really think your hammock will be strong enough to hold me and you?"
"I guarantee it."
"How about me and Tom Cruise?"

Paris and Throckmorton chatted with friends and left Matt alone to down shot after shot of gin. The warm glow intensified, expanding to a sense of universal understanding, ultimately building to an epiphany of communion with Billie Holiday. His eyes were half-closed as he grinned widely and mouthed along with Billie about how he simply "must have that man."

Applegate was transfixed. Matt seemed blissful and above it all, even enraptured; yet it was obvious that he was in tremendous pain. Applegate knew immediately it was a migraine. He was spellbound by the portrait of suffering amid the drugged ecstasy. Applegate wondered if that's how it was for Lady Day, if her eyes flashed with pain and despair as she gave birth to her musical rapture. He wondered if anyone is ever allowed to create art or think a noble thought without paying a terrible price.

It reminded Applegate of one of the unanticipated pleasures of his job: the opportunity to witness the incredible beauty that his clients radiate as they give themselves over to pain. In his sessions, Applegate could actually see the epiphany which overwhelms a migraine sufferer when they finally drop the dodges and drugs and denial and surrender completely to the agony—the surrender which, paradoxically, is the first and most important step in overcoming the pain.

Matthew was unmistakably wrestling with that surrender right now. The gin seemed to allow him to regulate the pain, to test the water and dip his toe into the abyss as much as he dared. When it got to be too much, another shot could anesthetize him, until he worked up the courage to try it again—rather like Applegate in a gay bar, drinking a beer to fortify himself, coming out of his reverie every so often to look around at the men in the bar with him, then having another beer when it became too threatening.

Matthew approached the surrender as the alcohol inhibited his fear and allowed him the courage to feel the migraine in all its fury. The post-migraine euphoria was already struggling to assert itself. Euphoria warred with pain and terror, all of it expressed clearly on the battlefield of Matthew's face. Applegate smiled as he studied the vast, gentle, brown eyes and child-like, trembling mouth.

Matthew's face contorted in agony as the migraine suddenly renewed its attack. Matt ceased drinking and allowed the pain to sweep over him in waves of terrifying anger and cruelty. Now the alcohol backfired on him, doubling the migraine, making him dizzy and disoriented. As the pain reached a crescendo, his face took on a look of calm and understanding; perhaps the same look on a mother's face at the moment of birth, as physical pain becomes aware of new life, as the suffering just begins to surrender to joy; perhaps the same look on Lady Day's face as she would strike a note of sublime beauty, transcending the horrors of her life and twisting them, suicidally, into something divine.

Or perhaps it was a look peculiar to Matthew, a look which only Applegate was able to perceive and appreciate, a secret union which was unique to them.

"It was about these World War II veterans who compare notes on the derrieres of their spouses. It was called *The Best Rears of our Wives*."

"Damn! Now my beer is warm!"
"Try holding it between your legs."

"It's tough, but it's not surmountable."

"What's your favorite opera?"
"I don't know. Probably the Macintosh."

"I'm telling you, he was an albino negro."

"I have the memory of an elephant."

"That's not all."

Lady Day once remarked that people came to her concerts in order to see her get so blitzed that she'd "fall into the damn orchestra pit." That line now seemed unbearably poignant to Applegate. It was said in jest, and yet there was an undercurrent of self-deprecation, a suggestion that people didn't really appreciate her talent but merely were intrigued by her persona. Or was Applegate reading too much into an innocent little joke?

Then Applegate recalled reading that once Billie threatened a sailor with a broken beer bottle when the sailor called her a "nigger". And just a few days later, she was heard saying to friends, "Well, you know, I'm still a nigger."

Applegate took a long guzzle of Weiss.

The contradictions of the human soul. The struggle to love one's self. All were now expressed in Matthew's face. Applegate thought of how migraine people are a strange group. They tend to blame themselves for their headaches. The subjectivity of a migraine makes it impossible to measure or record. Cholesterol can be assigned a number, tumors can be removed, germs can be isolated, while a migraine can only be felt. There is a stigma associated with having migraines, as if the sufferer is either insane or a crybaby. Friends and family invariably recommend, "Just take an aspirin and get on with your life." Migraine people internalize that attitude, denying their own pain and the very real horror of a migraine attack.

Applegate drained the glass.

Just as gay men tend to internalize the hatred of the society in which they live, just as all gay men must wrestle with self-hatred and contradictions. Some overcome it. Some triumph. Some engage in behavior they know will lead to AIDS and then use the disease to prove to themselves that they are an abomination and deserve to die. Some create art and literature, shaming the society which condemns them. Some revel in being a pariah. Some dedicate their lives to the human race. Even gay pornography is an assertion of the human spirit, a demand for recognition, a beacon of defiance—

A "beacon of defiance"? Applegate smiled and realized he must be drunk if he was using phrases like that. He came out of his daydream and looked around.

The bar had changed; it was radiant. For the second time in his life, the door had opened a crack. For the second time, Applegate was getting a glimpse of the inner palace. Yes, there was no doubt; the men here tonight—these strange creatures who lived on pale moonlight—were the people he was seeking. The door remained open for several seconds.

If only he could figure out how to approach them; they all seemed so foreign, so beautiful and exotic, so ethereal and divine… How could he talk to them without looking hopelessly naive and crude? What language did they speak? What world did they inhabit? If only he knew how to express it all to them. If only he knew what he wanted to express.

He saw two men near the window. They kissed each other. Applegate felt a stab of longing, a spasm of jealousy. The door had slammed shut.

As the final Billie Holiday song began, Applegate could almost hear a hush come over the crowd. He was sure it was his imagination; this group tonight was too boisterous to let a little music slow them down.

Applegate watched Matthew. Matt had stopped drinking now; his face was red, his eyes bleary. He looked as if he were about to fall into the damn orchestra pit.

Matthew struggled to his feet. Paris put an arm around his waist and helped him to the door. Applegate could hear Paris saying to Throckmorton, "It's late anyway and I have to work tomorrow; I'll take him home in a cab."

Throckmorton stroked Matthew's hair. "The poor baby." Then he fluttered his hands and said to Paris, "Call me tomorrow!"

Kisses all around as Paris said, "Don't forget lunch on Friday!"

Final kisses. "I can't wait! Mmmmmmm!"

"Come on, big boy."

As Paris dragged Matthew out the door, Throckmorton hissed to his companion, "I thought that bitch would never leave!"

TWENTY-TWO

Applegate and Dutchman were shopping on a blazing July afternoon. They walked into Radio Shack. A salesman asked if he could help them. Dutchman said, "I need a VCR. Can I finance one?"

"Sure. Do you have a Visa?"

"Yeah."

"Well, just give it to me. I'll run it through the computer, and we'll set up a Radio Shack account for you."

"I don't have it on me."

"No problem, bring it in next time."

"Okay." After a moment's silence, Dutchman asked, "What if I don't have a Visa?"

If the salesman was skeptical, he hid it well. "Just fill out an application with your place of employment and annual salary, and we can still open an account for you."

Out on the street Applegate asked in amazement, "What was that all about? You can't even pay your rent. How could you afford a VCR?"

"I don't know. Maybe Robert could pay for it."

"Who's Robert?"

"New roommate. I threw Calvin out."

This was the first Applegate had heard of the new living arrangement. "You did?"

"Yeah, I got tired of his bullshit."

"And all that about having a Visa! You don't have a Visa."

"I know. But maybe I could open a Radio Shack account."

"You don't have a job."

Dutchman was evasive. Applegate wondered if this was a case of AIDS-dementia, or if Dutchman was merely impractical. He thought it best not to pursue this topic right now.

Applegate asked, "How do you like living with Robert?"

"He's okay. He wants to be my lover."

"And you don't like that idea?"

"Last week he wanted to fuck, so I told him I didn't have any rubbers. He said to go get some."

"What did you do?"

"I went out for an hour and came back and told him the store was closed." Dutchman stared poker-faced at Applegate a moment. Then they both burst out laughing.

"Did he believe you?"

"He didn't say anything."

"You know, if you want, you could get a part-time job. You're well enough to work. I could help you find a job."

"I'll think about it. I saw Zack last week."

"A friend of yours?"

"My old lover. The one that gave me the AIDS."

"You know who gave you AIDS?"

"What do you think, that I used to hang around the baths? I only had four lovers in my life."

"And you're 25?"

"Yeah, only four lovers. I never fucked around with baths and bushes and that."

"How was Zack?"

"Like always."

Applegate wasn't sure what that meant. He asked, "When were you first diagnosed?"

"A year and a half ago. The week before Easter. I woke up in the hospital. That was a year after I broke up with Zack." Applegate tried to keep the dates straight. The virus had taken over a year to become active, maybe two or three years (depending on how long Zack and Dutchman had been lovers), a time frame within the normal range. Dutchman continued, "I saw him about a month before I got pneumonia, and he was laughing and asking me have I got it yet."

Applegate had difficulty controlling his emotions; he had difficulty comprehending what Dutchman was telling him.

"He was laughing? About what?"

"He just got out of the hospital. His doctors told him to warn his sex partners. He was laughing about giving me the AIDS."

"I don't get it."

Dutchman showed no emotion as he said, "There's nothing to get. He's a dick. He thought it was funny that he gave me the AIDS. He was smiling, asking me am I sick yet, have I been in the hospital yet."

"How... how did you feel when he said that?"

"It was too late to feel anything. I already had it."

Dutchman's tone told Applegate that this discussion was at its limit.

Back at Dutchman's apartment, Applegate said, "We had a workshop at the clinic. They told us about medical power of attorney. I thought you might like to get one."

Dutchman looked afraid, like the subject might be painful. He asked, "What's that?"

"Well, you appoint someone to be your medical power of attorney, and then if you get too sick to direct your own treatment, the person you appoint tells the doctors when to give you treatment and when to pull the plug."

"I thought we did that with the living will."

"It's extra protection to make sure your wishes are carried out. With the medical power of attorney, the doctor has someone there, who he knows you trust, to help him decide what to do."

"The doctor decides?"

"The living will and the medical power of attorney aren't the whole thing. Doctors can override them in some cases, especially since the doctors are the ones who determine your chance of recovery. And some doctors won't pull the plug no matter what, because of moral or legal ramifications."

"I just don't want to be feeling any pain. If I'm in pain, I want them to let me go."

"That's something you would discuss with the person you appoint."

"How about you?"

Applegate looked down to the floor. He had been afraid Dutchman would ask that question. "They told us in the workshop that we can't be appointed for our clients. Too many legal complications. You have to appoint a friend or family member."

There was an awkward silence. Applegate wasn't sure if Dutchman had anyone whom he trusted like that. None of Dutchman's friends would so much as witness his will; they felt that any talk of wills was morbid. Would they even consider taking on this new responsibility? Would any of Dutchman's family members come through for him?

Applegate felt a wave of despair as he contemplated the emptiness of Dutchman's life. In his training, Applegate had been told that AIDS doesn't change a person. On the contrary, it makes them more of what they already were. Loners become more introverted, the mildly religious become fervent, the optimistic increase their faith in life.

This rule was not inviolable. The trainer spoke of one client, HIV positive and a confirmed fatalist, who said that he wanted to commit suicide at the first sign of the onset of AIDS. That same client, when actually faced with death, became resolutely determined to live, fighting off one opportunistic disease after another, trying any treatment he could, tracking down rumors of new treatments, digging through medical journals and educating his doctors on the latest finds.

But in the vast majority of cases, AIDS made its victims become more intensely what they already were. Applegate thought back on all Dutchman had told him about his dysfunctional family, his selfish and uncaring friends, his unfulfilling romance with Calvin, his ambivalent relationship with his Baptist faith. There was no support in his life, no source of strength.

Dutchman had said that he hadn't gotten any visitors the last time he was in the hospital. It suddenly occurred to Applegate that Dutchman had had one visitor: Applegate. The profound loneliness of Dutchman's struggle, the isolation he had grown up in and was now going to die in–it all swept over Applegate in waves. Would Dutchman suffer? Would anyone besides Applegate be there for him? Would his family come to him when he got really sick? Or would AIDS make them more of what they were? Would the onset of death make them pull away further, just as they were pulling away now at the very possibility of death?

Applegate looked around at Dutchman's apartment, a nice little one-bedroom which reeked of loneliness and pain. They had warned him in training that there would be times when the suffering would become overwhelming, and at such times it was important to step back out of the situation. Applegate needed to do that now. He said to Dutchman, "Well, it's about time for me to get going. Let's think about that medical power of attorney. I'll ask my supervisor at the clinic if she has any ideas about who to name. Maybe your pastor or a church member. Is that possible?"

Dutchman nodded absently. He didn't say anything. Applegate went to hug him, as he often did when leaving. Dutchman held him close for many minutes.

TWENTY-THREE

Applegate hovered by the ceiling, drawing languidly on a pipe from the huge hookah. Jacques Hardoné lay on the bed. As Applegate half-closed his eyes to savor the latest rush, Jacques pointed the VCR remote control at him. A blue laser beam flickered between the unit and Applegate. Jacques moved the unit in his hand; the beam intensified and drew Applegate along with it across the room, seven feet above the floor.

There was strange music in the background, Buddhist ceremonial music consisting of unsettling melodies and unknown instruments. A deep, low flute evoked images of deserted fields and desolate sunsets. Applegate heard banjo sounds, but banjo unlike any he had ever experienced... a sort of psycho-banjo out of tune and out of control. In his altered state of mind, the bizarre music blended into a pleasing harmony, a warm bath of sweetly-scented water.

Jacques asked, "So it's not sex, is it?"

Applegate felt himself being pulled back from his Tibetan odyssey. It took several seconds to leave the music, but when he drank in the sight of Jacques stretched out below him on the bed, Applegate managed to focus his attention. "What's that? Not sex?"

"What you were afraid of."

Applegate sighed dreamily and declared, "Me? I've never been afraid of anything in my life."

"You said you were afraid of sex."

"Yeah, I thought I was. Am I?"

"You went home with Kevin."

"I wasn't afraid of him."

"Why not?"

"I don't know."

"You knew he wanted to sleep with you."

Applegate contemplated the memory of Kevin's eyes. "I knew it. I could tell right away."

"That's why you weren't afraid of him."

"But I thought I was afraid of sex."

"I thought you weren't afraid of anything."

"I used to be."

Jacques laughed. He gestured, and the window opened. Jacques used the remote control unit to guide Applegate, still floating, out the window. "You believed you were afraid of sex. What you're afraid of is intimacy. You could go home with Kevin because you knew there would never be any emotional bond between you. You could fuck him because you knew that after you did, you could forget him."

"I knew all that?"

"Of course. And that's why you were so scared of Matthew."

"Who?"

"Matthew. The guy who asked you what kind of beer you were drinking."

"His name is Matthew?" Applegate looked down; he was outside his bedroom window, levitating four floors above the street. As he gazed at the pavement below, he felt no fear. He was merely distracted by the unusual perspective he was getting of the familiar avenue. When he glanced up and noticed the blue laser connecting him with Jacques, he suddenly was reminded of their conversation. "His name is Matthew?"

Jacques was amused by Applegate's languid confusion. "Matthew. You were afraid of him because you knew he wanted more than sex. He was offering you intimacy. Emotional. Spiritual. Romantic."

"How did you know his name was Matthew?"

"You told me."

"But I didn't know it. I don't know anything about him."

"You probably overheard it. On a subconscious level. A little hashish brings it out, uncovers the sights and sounds you absorb in your everyday existence. And you whispered it to me. Without words."

"With Matt, I'd like... I'd like to talk to him."

"Instead of sex?"

Applegate thought a moment before answering, "During sex."

"That's my specialty!"

Applegate again looked down. Jacques laughed and tossed the VCR unit to him. Applegate reached out and caught it. As he did so, his body suddenly regained its weight. He felt his legs drop underneath him. He held onto the VCR unit, which remained stationary in the air. Applegate dangled, holding the unit with one hand. "Hey, what happened?"

Jacques smiled. "You have to concentrate on getting it up. You let it deflate. Concentrate on making it hard."

"On making what hard?"

Jacques pursed his lips and said, "Just keep thinking, 'I can feel it rising. I can feel it rising.' Sort of like 'There's no place like home.' Only more interesting."

Applegate clicked his heels three times, repeating "I can feel it rising." On the third click, his feet levitated to the height of the remote control. Applegate floated on his back, holding the unit over his head. He wiggled his toes and floated into the room. He used his free hand as a rudder and landed next to Jacques on the bed.

Jacques said, "Very good. You've got the hang of it."

"Yeah, it's hanging long and easy."

"That's the spirit. So what about Matthew?"

"His name is Matthew?"

"You told me."

"Right."

$\mathcal{T}$WENTY-FOUR

Even before the last of the applause had died down, Elyssia's phone rang. She turned off the T.V. and picked up the receiver.

She knew who it would be. "Hello, Applegate."

"CAN THAT SON OF A BITCH SING OR WHAT!!!!?????"

Elyssia laughed and began to say, "Yes, he was in fine voice," but she knew that Applegate would be doing most of the talking.

"Did you hear how he sang the motherfucker '*Che Gelida Manina*'????!!!!!!!"

Applegate so rarely used profanity that it amused Elyssia when he did. He was obviously very drunk. He was also more than a little enraptured by Luciano Pavarotti, who had just completed a concert on public television.

"Jesus fucking Christ!!!!! Did you hear what he did with '*O Solo Mio*'?"

"A traditional favorite—"

"'*Nessun Dorma*'! '*Nessun* cocksucking *Dorma*'!!!!!!"

"Well, I don't know much about opera, but I did enjoy the way he kept hitting that one note—"

"HIGH C!!!!!! HIGH C!!!!!!!"

Elyssia nodded and said, "That Pavarotti is one bad motherfucker."

TWENTY-FIVE

It was 12:30 on a Sunday night. Applegate had no appointments scheduled for tomorrow. He thought back on the weekend–it had been barren. This coming Saturday was his 30th birthday.

He'd drunk maybe a six-pack. He considered going to bed. After agreeing on the sanity of such a course and the total lunacy of drinking any more, he got dressed, ran down the stairs and hailed a cab.

"Addison and Halsted, please."

The driver dropped him off in front of the Vortex.

He had never been here before. There was some sort of drag show going on in the main room. Applegate remained in the little bar adjoining it. He sat there, keeping an eye on the stage in the next room, sipping his Rolling Rock.

Applegate gradually noticed that two different men were discretely studying him. He realized that he had been unconsciously making eye contact with both.

The first was short, bald, thin and the most intriguing man in the bar. He seemed to be on excellent terms with everyone. Several men called out to him, and most of the drag performers stopped and chatted. Yet he was alone. Applegate was enthralled by his friendliness and enthusiasm.

Enthralled, that is, until he got a good look at the second man several stools down from the first. Applegate did not like to think of himself as a shallow person. He envisioned himself as actuated by the spirit, not the body. But when he looked at Raymond, a certain chest and a certain smile obliterated all awareness of the metaphysical.

Raymond smiled at Applegate and took a long drink from his beer, finishing his stein in one gulp. Applegate smiled and gave a slight wave of his hand. He tried to appear nonchalant, but he was like a cat watching a sparrow: the muscles sculptured, but the tail wagging berserk.

Raymond walked up to Applegate, tapped him on the chest, pointed to a flamboyantly painted queen nearby and said, "She's a lovely person."

Applegate smiled, "I'm sure she is."

"No! Really! She's a lovely person!" His eyes were glazed and his speech slurred.

"I believe you. She looks very nice."

Raymond announced proudly, "I gotta piss. I'll be right back."

Applegate turned again to the stage, wondering if Raymond would come back and talk some more. After a few minutes, he was at Applegate's shoulder. He nodded and sat down.

Applegate asked, "So what's your name?"

He extended his hand. "Raymond."

"Applegate."

Raymond kissed Applegate's hand. "Enchanted. Hey, I'm a little broke. Will you buy me a beer?"

"Sure." Applegate signalled, and the bartender brought over two Rolling Rocks.

"I'm from Michigan."

"Really. What brings you to Chicago?"

"I come down every few months for a week or two, you know, cruising the gay bars. And I never miss the Halsted Street Fair."

"Which bars do you like?"

Raymond sipped his beer. "Oscar's mostly."

"That's a bar for female impersonators, isn't it?"

Raymond seemed very sad for a moment. Finally he said, "Yeah."

Applegate gathered there was some sort of story having to do with Raymond and a queen, but he didn't want to pry. Instead he asked, "What do you do in Michigan?"

"I breed dogs."

"No kidding. What kind?"

"Shar-Peis."

"Shar-Peis? Which are they?"

Raymond smiled. "Glad you asked. I just happen to have a picture–" He took out his wallet and showed Applegate a dozen photos.

Applegate said, "Oh, very handsome Very wrinkled."

"Raising Shar-Peis is a ludicrous business."

"You mean you don't like it?"

"No, I mean there's a lot of money in it."

Applegate wondered if he meant "lucrative", but only said, "I see."

"My roommate's gonna kill me."

"Why?"

"I been here two weeks. I was supposed to be back three days ago. I haven't called him. He's gonna kill me."

"What's he like?"

"Florindo? He's an older guy. Owns the house. Owns the kennel, too."

Applegate began to form the picture of a young drifter kept by an older man. It appeared that Raymond was prolonging his binge to avoid a confrontation.

"Where are you staying?"

"Ain't got no place right now."

Applegate had expected that answer. Was Raymond just looking for a place to sleep?

"I sold my body lots of times." Applegate looked at Raymond. Raymond would have no problem finding a bed; he was beautiful. Dark, hairy, swarthy; well-defined face and lovely eyes. He was a little shorter than Applegate and solid muscle. Applegate would have guessed him to be 25 years old.

"Yeah, I been a hustler, mostly when I was younger."

"How old are you?"

"Thirty-nine."

"You're kidding!"

"No, thirty-nine, Vietnam vet."

"You could pass for twenty-five."

Raymond looked bored as he said, "Yeah, I know." He reached up and put his hand through Applegate's hair. "You have nice hair. Is it really yours?"

Perhaps a peculiar question. But if the gesture was meant to arouse Applegate, it worked handsomely.

"Sure it's mine. Do you like it?"

Raymond brought his hand down to the back of Applegate's neck and rested it there several moments. "It's really wonderful, soft and curly."

"So is yours." Applegate reached out and massaged Raymond's thick chest hair spilling over the top of his low-cut undershirt. "Thick and shiny." Raymond laughed. Applegate tugged, "Is this real?"

"Everything about me is real." Raymond's smile was brilliant white.

An hour later, Applegate and Raymond were in Snack-N-Dine, an all-night diner close to Applegate's apartment. Raymond was saying, "Yeah, I was over there for two years. Saw a lot of my buddies get blown away. Killed a few people myself. Not proud of it."

"I feel like... Did you ever meet someone who's your opposite, and yet you know there's a bond? I mean, I've never been to war, but–"

Raymond reached across the table and took Applegate's hand. "You've been to war, Applegate. I can tell. Some personal kind of war. And you've been wounded."

Applegate's voice was unsteady as he whispered, "Well, yeah, a sort of war..."

"Why do you think I spoke to you tonight? I knew who you were the moment I laid eyes on you. I knew you'd understand about Vietnam. I never talk about it. You're the first person in years..." He smiled and kissed Applegate on the cheek. "That's okay, baby, you let it out. That's okay."

"I like you, Raymond. I really like you a lot."

"I like you, too. I want you to come up to Michigan sometime. Spend the weekend. I want to pay you back for the beers and the food. You'll love it. Florindo and I have a big house. You'll have your own room." After a moment he said impishly, "If you want your own room." Applegate laughed. "I'll give you a massage like you'll never forget. We can go bike riding down this path I know, 50 miles past corn fields, ponds, cattle grazing..."

"Sounds wonderful."

Raymond leaned back and sighed, "It's so peaceful in Michigan. You'll feel reborn. It will heal all the hurt inside you."

Applegate said earnestly, "Oh, Raymond, I wish I could invite you to stay with me tonight. I really do..." After his experience with Kevin, Applegate was determined never to spend the night with a stranger.

"No, I understand. But I'll write to you. We'll get to know each other. We'll take it one step at a time. I can wait." He nodded and smiled. "I can wait."

"When are you going back to Michigan?"

"Tomorrow morning first thing."

"Will you be back soon?"

"Florindo and I are coming down for the Cubs game Saturday."

"Really? This Saturday?"

"Yeah. Want to meet me afterwards? Like for dinner?"

"Saturday is my birthday."

"No kidding?" Raymond kissed Applegate's hand. "May I be your escort for that very special evening?"

"Uh, yeah... yeah..."

"Tell you what, the game will be over by 5:00 or 6:00. Want to meet me at 7:00?"

"Sure, great."

"Do you know Buddies?"

"Yeah, down Halsted."

"We'll meet at Buddies, 7:00 o'clock, this Saturday. It's a date?"

"Sure, I won't forget."

Apparently somebody forgot something. It was 8:00 o'clock and no Raymond. Applegate wasn't surprised. Raymond hadn't called all week, hadn't answered his phone in Michigan. Maybe he hadn't gone back at all. Applegate knew from the first that Raymond was alcoholic and unreliable. But Raymond was so beautiful, so warm... and so drunk last week he probably had no memory of their conversation.

Applegate alternated between feeling sorry for the poor alcoholic lost in a maze of forgotten promises and feeling furious at the whore who had played with his emotions for a place to sleep.

Applegate was sitting at the bar, at the window which overlooked the street. He was hoping he might catch a glimpse of Raymond rushing to the door. It suddenly struck him that he had regressed to his Madame Butterfly persona.

He had described to Dr. Bellman, years ago when he began psychoanalysis, that the opera *Madama Butterfly* held a ghastly fascination for him. Not simply because it was full of pain and rejection, but particularly for the waiting scene where Butterfly spends the entire night, from dusk until dawn, looking out the window, waiting in vain for her husband to come home to her. Applegate had told Dr. Bellman how Butterfly's frustration epitomized all of his dealings with men.

And now, looking out onto Halsted, Applegate was reliving that scene, was reliving a part of his life he thought he had left behind. Applegate jumped from the chair and ran out of the bar. He would never go back to that. He would never return to the time of the migraines and the hallucinations and the Butterfly anguish. He'd spent too much time in analysis, suffered too dearly for his sanity, to ever allow those times to return.

He charged down the street in a fury. He thought back to fifteen years of migraine headaches, headaches which had driven him to attempt suicide. He thought of the filthy, nauseating hallucinations he had experienced whenever he felt desire for a man: the phantom cockroaches crawling under his clothes, the stifling smell of excrement.

Then he focused on the source of all those horrors; he recalled the consummate fiend. For years he had blocked out conscious memory of his father's abuse. It wasn't until Dr. Bellman had provided him with a "safe environment" that Applegate had been able to allow the memories to return.

For the first year of analysis, Dr. Bellman had repeated to Applegate that he was safe when they were together, that Applegate could face all the devils of hell in this room and nothing could hurt him. Applegate, in denial, had no idea what the doctor was talking about.

But after that first year, after a bond was firmly established between Applegate and Bellman, the memories began to assert themselves. They were over-whelming: scenes of rape, scenes of sexual humiliation, scenes of torture with razor blades and lit cigarettes. Some memories presented themselves all in an instant; some took weeks to form. Images and half-memories which had haunt-ed him all his life now fleshed out to real-life nightmares.

As he was able to remember more and more of what had happened to him as a child, the migraines and hallucinations quickly subsided. This gave Apple-gate little comfort at the time. Often he felt that he would rather suffer the migraines than face the bitter reality–reality made a thousand times worse by his awareness that these horrors were not in the past. Now it was other chil-dren–unfamiliar pictures in the newspapers, twisted faces on television–but it was the same horror, still alive and active, still vast and pervasive.

But he had gotten through it. He had reached the point where Dr. Bellman had told him he was strong enough to face the world on his own. He was help-ing migraine sufferers, he was bringing comfort to AIDS patients. But was he ready to live in the present? Was he ready to deal with the world on its own terms? What was in that world for him? What if no one ever responded? What if he always remained an outsider?

Applegate now found himself in Oscar's, Raymond's favorite bar. Already drunk, he became more so. A gaudily made-up queen approached him. "Hi, baby, my name is Madelaine."

Applegate looked at the young man. It was a strange face he saw, but it was smiling. The smile was enough to make Applegate talkative. "Hi, Madalyn, I'm Applegate. Can I buy you a drink?"

Madelaine brought a hand to her cheek and shyly said, "I'd be enchanted with a cognac. But my name is 'Ma-de-LANE', not 'MAD-a-lin'."

"I apologize. Bartender! A cognac for the lovely Madelaine!"

Applegate asked her, "So what brings you here tonight?"

Madelaine sighed like Tallulah Bankhead, "I'm bored and looking for a good time. How about you?"

"I'm looking for Raymond."

"Raymond?"

"From Michigan. Raises Shar-Peis. Do you know him?"

Madelaine said demurely, "No, I don't believe I do."

The alcohol turned bitter. "You've probably fucked him. Everybody's fucked Raymond."

Madelaine's eyes flashed. With her hand on her hip she threw her head back and spit out, "Honey, I don't fuck everybody who everybody fucks!" With that she swished away, cognac in hand.

Applegate had no doubt that Raymond and Madelaine had been lovers. He pictured Raymond kissing Madelaine. He called after her, "Whore! Fucking lousy whore! I know you've had him! I bet every bitch in this bar had Raymond!"

The music was loud enough to all but drown him out. In disgust, Applegate threw his bottle of beer to the floor and ran outside. He hailed a cab.

"Take me to the Blue Gardenia!"

"Blue Gardenia? Down Halsted?"

"Just take me there and shut up."

"Jeez…"

In the Blue Gardenia, Applegate worked on getting more drunk and more bitter. As he sucked on the bottle he watched the happy young men touching each other. He looked at the smiling faces in the porno videos. No one had ever smiled at him in bed. The closest he'd ever come to making love was being raped by his father. No wonder he was so fucked up. Could it ever be healed? Could he ever straighten himself out? Dr. Bellman thought so. But Dr. Bellman had abandoned him too. Applegate wasn't ready to be on his own. Why had Bellman insisted he was? Every man he had ever wanted had betrayed him. And now, on his thirtieth birthday, he was stood up by the nicest man he had ever met.

Was there any way out? Was there anything he could do to break through?

He looked up. There was a familiar face in the distance. He tried to see through the haze. It was that guy… that guy who had approached him that time, that guy who asked him what kind of beer he was drinking.

No, it wasn't him. It just looked like him.

Applegate pondered the effect that face had on him. That face had made the door open. Twice. Yes, there was a way out. That guy… Matthew! Jacques Hardoné had told him the guy's name was Matthew! Matthew had opened the door, had shown Applegate the inner palace.

He studied the face at the end of the bar. He concentrated on it until he convinced himself it was Matthew. He fought his way through the crowd and up to the stranger.

Applegate called out, "Matthew! You're Matthew!"

The stranger looked him up and down. "You're stinking drunk."

"Jacques Hardoné told me your name is Matthew!"

"Jock Hard-on the porno star?"

"Yeah! We were flying!"

"Flying?"

"In my bedroom!"

With disgust the stranger said, "Get lost, asshole!"

"Aren't you Matthew? Don't you like me?"

He snarled, "My name is Pinkerton."

Applegate laughed. "That Jacques! He was putting me on!"

"I told you, get lost. You're drooling on my shoes."

"But Matthew–"

"Pinkerton!"

"Whatever you are!" Applegate grabbed Pinkerton's arm. "I love you!"

"Let go of me! I'm warning you!"

Applegate let go and stepped back. Was it Matthew? The eyes were different than he remembered. But the beer churning in his stomach lied to him and told him that Pinkerton was the man.

Or perhaps it was something far more insidious than alcohol. Applegate's subconscious had for years been producing confusion and terror in order to protect him from intimacy. Perhaps mistaking Pinkerton for Matthew was one final attempt to sabotage any chance for salvation; one last, dying gasp of the childhood abuse which still mistook romance for rape.

Applegate had no awareness of the conflicting forces within him. He knew only one truth, and he yelled it at Pinkerton, "But you opened the door for me! No one else ever did that. You showed me the palace."

"I'm going to show you my fist in a minute. Why don't you be a good boy and go open that door over there? On the other side you'll find a nice yellow cab—"

The frustration of thirty years welled up and erupted. "God damn it I love you! You're the one. You're the one who opened the door!" When Pinkerton turned his back on Applegate, Applegate punched him on the shoulder.

It was a clumsy, glancing blow, but Pinkerton got off his stool, faced Applegate and said, "Now I'm gonna cut your ass—" He produced a switchblade from his jacket. The knife sprung open with a twanging sound.

With the bitterness of a spurned lover, Applegate reached down and grabbed the pearl-encased keychain canister of tear gas. He held it up. "Keep back! Once I open this—" He fumbled to release the safety catch. A stream of tear gas shot down to the floor, grazing Pinkerton's trousers.

The chemical was so potent that even the fumes were enough to make Pinkerton fall back on the floor and cover his face. He scrambled to his feet and retreated to the wall. A few other customers were becoming aware of the ruckus.

Applegate looked at them all staring back at him with vague fear on their faces, vague curiosity and vague indifference. In a grand passion of drunken self-pity he cried out, "Don't worry! I'm leaving! I won't bother any of you, ever again! Damn you all! You're no better than my old man! He was right! You're all just like him…"

He focused on Pinkerton. Applegate beheld the interior of a shining, opulent palace which would never be his. He saw a vast golden door slamming in his face. "I love you!"

Pinkerton sneered, "Fucking psycho!"

"Oh, go to hell! All of you!" Applegate was out the door and into a cab before anyone could respond.

TWENTY-SIX

Applegate did not regress to what he had been.

When he woke up the next afternoon, he noticed that there was a message on his answering machine. He hadn't heard it ring because he had unplugged the phone. He didn't remember unplugging the phone, but there it was with the cord wrapped around the receiver. He always unplugged the phone when he came in drunk.

He pressed the play button. Elyssia's voice said, "Applegate? Are you there? Applegate? Do you hate men? Do you hate the world? Do you hate me? Do you hate yourself? You called me last night. You probably don't remember. Call me when you have the strength to dial the phone. We'll talk about it, okay? God bless."

Applegate smiled. He had a vague recollection...

He picked up the phone and dialed Dr. Bellman's answering service. "Hi, I'd like to leave a message for Dr. Bellman. My name is Jerry Applegate. Please tell him I'd like– No, please tell him I need to see him today. He can call and leave a message on my machine, and I'll be there whatever time he has available. I won't be home, so please be sure he leaves the message on my machine."

Applegate got dressed and left his apartment. It was late July. He wandered the streets. He went into bookstores and spent more money than he should. He ate at a little ethnic diner. He ate a great deal. He hardly thought at all. He called his answering machine every 20 minutes. Within two hours, Dr.

Bellman had left a message to meet him at 6:00 p.m.

When he got to Dr. Bellman's office, Applegate felt hollow and psychotic.

He gave Bellman a brief run-down of the previous night and then said, "I kept thinking that you were the enemy, that you had betrayed me."

"By telling you that you were strong enough to face the world?"

"Yeah."

"You felt I had abandoned you?"

"Like you had cast me out because you didn't want me, just like no gay man wants me."

The doctor observed, "This isn't the first time you've seen me as the enemy."

Applegate thought about it. "When... when I started... sometimes you looked..." Applegate was silent several moments.

"When you started in analysis, there were several times you hallucinated."

"I saw you as demonic. Just like my father. Like you had turned into him. I saw this room as filthy."

"We're dealing with the transference. When something bad happens to you, you tend to ascribe it to me. This is normal. I'm glad you came to see me today."

"Me too. I knew right away when I woke up that you hadn't betrayed me. I don't think Raymond did either. I think he's just an innocent drunk who really likes me but forgot all about me when I was out of his sight."

"He sounds harmless enough. Not like Pinkerton."

Applegate shuddered at the memory of Pinkerton holding the switchblade. "No, he's a real psycho." He thought about it a second and said, "Look who's talking!"

"No, Applegate, you're not a psycho. But Pinkerton sounds very dangerous. I hope you've gotten over your crush on him."

"Completely! When I think of the things I said last night... telling that man I loved him! How could I have thought such a thing?"

"Obviously his presence inspired a lot of intense feelings in you. You're not crazy, you're just inexperienced. Perhaps you're moving too fast again."

"Know what I think I'll do? I think I'll stay away from the Halsted strip for a while. If I go out to a bar, I'll go to one that's not in the Halsted/Roscoe area. Maybe like down by Carol's. You know, and just observe like I used to when I first started going to gay bars. Stand there and watch the guys touching each other. Like before Pinkerton came up to me and asked me what kind of beer I was drinking."

"How is your work with Dutchman going?"

"Real good. He was pretty sick a while back, but the crisis seems to be over. For now at least."

"You find a great deal of purpose in your relationship with him."

"Just like my migraine consulting. I feel like you healed me, and now I want to heal other people." Applegate thought a moment and then said, "It's like you have some magic power that you passed onto me, and now I want to use it for other people."

"That's a very great compliment. Even though–"

"I know, you didn't really heal me, you just showed me how to heal myself. Yeah, we've been through this a dozen times. All I'm saying is you have a gift."

Dr. Bellman laughed. "And now you feel like you have it too?"

"Well, yeah, sort of. I mean, I'm trying. I'll tell you, Dutchman's a real challenge. He's in this roller coaster relationship with Calvin. One week he throws him out. The next Calvin is back, and Dutchman is saying that they're lovers just trying to make it in the world. My supervisor at the clinic thinks it's AIDS dementia."

"What do you think?"

"It seems like plain old denial like I see in my migraine clients. And a lot of times, Dutchman deliberately provokes Calvin. Like when we were making out his will, Dutchman called out to Calvin, 'We're making out my will.' You know, like a little kid would say to another to taunt him."

"How would that taunt Calvin?"

"Because Dutchman knew that Calvin thinks all talk of wills is morbid. And at that party, Dutchman was carrying on with Philip just to get a rise out of Calvin. And then when he does, when Calvin makes a scene, Dutchman complains about that."

"Maybe he's trying to drive Calvin away."

"I'll tell you, it's real difficult. I don't want to control his life, but I don't like this Calvin character. I don't want to come out and say that. I think Dutchman knows how I feel. I don't really know how I feel. Right now, Calvin is back living with his mother, and Dutchman's apartment is overrun with friends coming and going, some of them living there…"

Applegate hesitated. Dr. Bellman prompted, "But?"

"But… I mean, they're not really his friends. They're just using him for a free place to stay. At his birthday party last March, they were smoking. Smoking cigarettes, when he could barely breathe. None of them visited him when he was in the hospital last June. But Dutchman's so afraid of being alone. He's terrified of death. And I think he's getting sicker… I think he's surrounding himself with shallow, loveless people because he's afraid that if he's alone he'll think about dying."

"You see yourself in Dutchman. When you began to remember the abuse, the first thing you did was move away from your family."

"I do identify with Dutchman. I wish he'd break away from his so-called friends. Like I got away from my family. He needs to find real friends."

"Like you?"

"But I'm not exactly his friend. Sometimes I don't know my role. I'm his friend. But I'm assigned to be his friend, which is crazy. We have a professional relationship. But I love him."

"It's possible to love a client."

Applegate looked at Dr. Bellman. Both men felt that it was an important moment in their relationship.

"I don't know what to do for Dutchman because… because he's dying. He can't last much longer. He's too skinny, and he's losing weight… "

"Dutchman's not the only one who can't deal with his impending death."

"But… Am I doing any good for him? Does it mean anything, since he's going to die anyway? How am I helping him?"

"We're all going to die."

"But Dutchman will die sooner than you or me."

"You don't know that. You never know that. All life is transitory. None of us knows when we're going to die. We just have to do the best we can with our time."

Applegate didn't speak for several moments. He seemed very confused. Dr. Bellman said, "I think you need to ask yourself what you want out of your involvement with the clinic. Why are you doing this work? What attracted you to it in the first place."

"Those aren't easy questions."

"They're not intended to be."

"Maybe he'll get better? Like he always says he will?"

"Not very likely. I work with many AIDS patients myself."

"If Dutchman dies–"

"You'll continue to live. You'll get another client and start again. To do anything else would be to surrender to death."

$\mathcal{T}$WENTY-SEVEN

Me: 24, swimmer's build, brown hair, brown eyes. You: 30 to 40, handsome, hairy, mustache, independent–

Exotic enema sensations! For guys who want to "spill their guts"!

Auditions! Come try out for the lead in my personal "Love Story"! The work is hard, and it would help if you are too!

Hot? Work out and it shows? Professional? Want to meet same?

Browsing through the personals was much safer than cruising the bars. And some of the ads seemed sincere and intriguing.

GWM, 31, Roman Catholic, engineer, enjoys ballet, skiing, square dance. Seeks similar for friendship/possible romance.

That fit Applegate fairly well. He had left the Catholic faith a decade ago and had renounced Christianity two years later, preferring his own form of agnosticism, but he would have a lot in common with a man who had been raised Catholic. He loved ballet and square dance and had always wanted to go skiing...

He'd think about it some more. He resumed reading the ads.

> Hi, my name is Phil, and I believe life must be approached with passion–
>
> Hot jocks with big cocks needed by–
>
> Keneau Reeves type, very into basketball, seeking sensual River Phoenix clone for our own private Idaho.
>
> Enjoy reading and film noir?
>
> I'm seeking a well-endowed, gorgeous man, 25-30, financially successful, executive, Mel Gibson type–

Applegate assumed that most of us were seeking such a man.

> I want a committed relationship with a caring, sensitive individual who has evolved beyond stereotypes and middle-class morality. No fats, no fems, no one under 25, no suburbanites, no unemployeds, no blacks, Hispanics or Orientals. Sincere responses only. Send photo.
>
> Plow my ass!
>
> I like smooth, round buns, big hard muscles, all packed in spandex bike shorts.
>
> Need a big hairy man? Let me be your jellyroll baby!

Applegate decided to place an ad of his own in *Gay Chicago Magazine*. He got out some paper and jotted down:

> GWM, 30 YO, inexperienced, seeks same for mutual support, coming out issues. I enjoy working out, bar hopping, going to brunch. Call Jerry

The magazine would supply an audio box number for him to retrieve his messages. That way, he could hear responses to his ad on the voice mail, but no one would know how to reach him directly.

TWENTY-EIGHT

"Do you like this outfit on me?"

"Yes, it's very nice."

"Just very nice?"

"What?"

"Well, last time, you said my outfit was fabulous."

"Chardonnay, even if I thought your outfit was fabulous, I wouldn't say that. It would be inappropriate."

"Well, maybe you didn't say the word 'fabulous', but I could tell by the way your face lit up that you were thinking 'fabulous'. This time your face says 'okay'."

Applegate carefully tried to follow her line of thought. "'Okay'?"

"Yeah, 'okay'. So what's wrong with this outfit? Why don't you like it?"

He studied her. "It's very nice, really."

"It makes me look like a nun, doesn't it?"

"Now that you mention it—"

"Really? You think I look like a nun?"

"Well, as close as you'll ever—"

"Just because of the high collar?"

Applegate said, "I think it's more the black-and-white motif. But can we get on with our—"

"What's wrong with black and white?"

"Nothing! Nothing is wrong with black and white!"

"You said it's a nun's outfit."

Applegate's voice seemed to rise an octave, "Some nuns are very attractive. Mary Tyler Moore played a nun once. Jill St. John was a nun in *The Trouble with Angels.* I love that movie."

"I've seriously considered joining the convent... when I was a little girl."

"How were the headaches this week?"

"Are you saying my migraines are caused by a repressed desire to go into religious life?"

Applegate resorted to the standard response which he used whenever a conversation got incomprehensible: "In what sense?"

As always, the question caused Chardonnay to stop and think. Finally she asked, "Do you like these boots?"

"They're rather elaborate."

"I call them my birth control boots. By the time we unlace them, we've lost interest. Eric and I had a fight."

"Your gay friend?"

"Yeah. He says I owe him sixty dollars."

"For what?"

Chardonnay sounded absolutely incredulous, "Cleaning his rug."

"Why does he want you to pay for cleaning his rug?"

"He thinks I threw up on it."

"Why does he think that?"

"Well, I sort of did. Just on the corner."

"Were you drinking?"

"With Eric? What else?"

"You threw up on his rug, and he wants you to pay for cleaning it?"

"Yeah! The fuck-head. He's a real nut about cleanliness. I think it's part of his stream of consciousness or something."

Applegate tried to remain neutral. "Not wanting to live with vomit isn't exactly being a nut. Was it an expensive rug?"

"How should I know? It's one of those Orientals."

"Well, if you're going to throw up on rugs, I suppose it's your responsibility–"

"Do nuns drink a lot?"

"I never thought about it."

"If I never had sex, I'd be drunk all the time."

"Then perhaps it's better that you didn't go into religious life."

"Do you think I should pay him?"

"You mean Eric? For the rug?"

"You sometimes have a hard time keeping track of a conversation."

"In what sense?"

After a few moments, Chardonnay continued, "My friend Wolfgang called me the other day. I haven't seen him in eight months."

"What did he say?"

"I don't care what he said. I know what he wanted."

"What did he want?"

"He just wanted to get laid."

Applegate was intrigued. "He calls you out of the blue after eight months and expects sex?"

"Yeah."

"What did you tell him?"

"To come over tomorrow at eight."

"Do you think that's wise?"

"What do you mean?"

"If you don't know him well, you have to be concerned about AIDS. And there's the question of your self-esteem."

"Self esteem? You think maybe I have low self-esteem?"

"All I'm saying is, when two people relate to each other only sexually, that sometimes indicates they're afraid of true intimacy."

"Afraid of intimacy? That's possible…"

Applegate was impressed; this was the longest he and Chardonnay had ever managed to have a coherent conversation. "I'm no psychologist, but sex is often used as a substitute for conversation and communication when people are afraid to expose themselves."

Chardonnay seemed excited. "You know what I just realized?"

"What?"

"Last week, I bought a new issue of *Rolling Stone*, and I just realized–"

"Yes?"

"That I haven't seen it since! I bet I left it in the store!"

"In the store?"

"Damn! After paying all that money!"

"Yes, well…"

"Did I ever tell you about my first date with him?"

"With Wolfgang?"

"Who else?"

"Well, I… I mean…"

"It was a blind date. And he brought me to this fabulous party. It was elegant: men in tuxedos, women in gowns… some men in gowns, too. And lots of champagne. In this central room they had something like 200 champagne glasses arranged on a table. Two hundred or more on a mirrored table under this crystal chandelier. Man, you should have heard the crash!"

"Were you injured?"

"Fuck no, I got out of the way. But I was pretty loaded by the time we left.

And my fuck-head brother!"

"What did he do?"

"When Wolfgang brought me to the door, my brother said 'Thanks for bringing her inside; most of them just leave her in the bushes.'"

"But you've slept with him since then?"

"Yeah. At least, we try to. A lot of times he's like Shakespeare: full of sound and fury, and then petering out.

"Yes, Shakespeare was notorious for his problem with impotency."

Chardonnay laughed. Applegate wasn't sure why. After Applegate made more attempts to discuss her migraine problem, Chardonnay dismissed his comments and said, "I found out what was blocking my drain."

"You mentioned last time that you were having problems."

"It was awful! The plumber came and put some chemical down it. It stank like you can't believe. Just being in the apartment made my eyes burn. And the crud that got unearthed! Thick, black crud everywhere–"

"Okay, I get the idea!"

"And it was my contacts."

"I beg your pardon?"

Chardonnay looked at him pityingly. "My contact lenses. That's what was blocking the drain."

"Your contact lenses? Two little lenses–"

"No! They were in their case!"

"How stupid of me."

"So what do you think?"

"About what?"

"Should I wear them?"

"The lenses?"

Chardonnay shook her head. "Of course the lenses."

"They've been sitting in black crud for how long?"

"Two years."

"They've been sitting in black crud for two years. They've been exposed to a chemical so toxic that it burned your eyes just being in the same apartment, and now you want to put them into your eyes?"

"But I washed them."

Applegate thought to himself, "Probably in bleach!" Then he said aloud to her, "Well, it's your decision, but I wouldn't wear them. Especially since your prescription has probably changed in two years."

"Well, yeah."

"Have you made up your mind yet on how to tell your mother you're going to drop out of dental hygiene school?"

"Not that I know of."

TWENTY-NINE

"Dinner at eight!"

Guildenstern looked excitedly at Rosencrantz. "A dinner party? Tonight?"

"And we're the guests of honor!"

"Formal?"

"No, but I feel like dressing up."

"Would false antennae be pretentious?"

"Let's do it. I believe I'll lengthen mine by a quarter inch or so."

"I have some body polish that's very good."

"I love a smooth, shiny, black back." Rosencrantz looked down his little cockroach nose as he said, "Fuzzy brown is okay for everyday, but on special occasions, one likes to strut."

"Inch-long antennae, shiny body... what's the occasion?"

"A few close friends getting together."

"How very delightful. How relaxed and sophisticated. Who will be in attendance? Anyone we know?"

"He said six altogether. I'm sure Elyssia will be there. Probably faces we've seen before."

"Charming. Arranged around that little table? How cozy. How very droll it all sounds."

"He's a fabulous cook. Said something about artichokes. This is the season for them. I'm sure there'll be fresh flowers for a centerpiece, and if I know Applegate, there'll be hollandaise and poached fish, and strawberries and custard."

"Strawberries and custard! Lovely!"

Rosencrantz said, "He was getting out those crystal candlesticks."

"What atmosphere there'll be!"

"Wine glasses."

"Tall or squat?"

Rosencrantz's non-functional wings flared with emotion as he said, "Tall, with a subtle line of gold gently spiraling along the sides."

"Coy! Extremely coy!"

"Linen napkins…"

"Elegant. What time shall we arrive?"

Rosencrantz rolled onto his back and began absent-mindedly grooming himself as he philosophized, "Well, that's a good question. With six people we have to be careful. If we just go sauntering up the table leg and strolling over the appetizer, one of them is bound to smash us."

"That would put a crimp in the evening."

"Not to mention a stain on the tablecloth. I think we should arrive before the guests and… wait for them."

"Interesting."

Rosencrantz stopped grooming suddenly, leaving three legs sticking straight up in the air, and sat up on his tailbone, leaning forward intently. "If, say, you were stationed in the breadbasket on the underside of one of those fabulous brioche rolls he makes–"

"With the egg glaze?"

Rosencrantz jumped up onto all eight legs and stage-whispered into Guildenstern's auditory orifice, "Picture it: the delicate tongues of candle flame reflecting off the shiny crust, as Hillary or Samantha or Mr. Elaine–or whoever!–takes a tiny, scrumptious bite. The flaky crumbs cling to her lips, her free hand reaches up with her napkin, she dabs demurely, comments on how wonderful the roll is, holds it out to admire–"

Guildenstern's tiny cockroach shoulders trembled. "And who will be smiling back at her an inch away from her thumb but yours truly!"

"In the ensuing melee you'll be able to run across the table before anyone has the presence of mind to act. You might even be able to leave a leg or two on a plate."

"I love to do that! What better reminder, what more personal calling card, than a stray body part?"

Rosencrantz looked as excited as a schoolboy as he rubbed his two front legs together and said, "Now, here's an idea I've been playing with for some time. After dinner, he likes to entertain in the den. I suppose he might have candles in there also, but usually he turns on the lamp. Now, if I were on the inside of the shade–"

"With the bulb behind you!"

"Think of the shadow I'll cast onto the opposite wall!"

Guildenstern gasped in awe, "A four-foot cockroach!"

Rosencrantz got up on his hind legs, spread his other legs wide and pronounced, "A show-stopper!"

"Ominous! Forbidding! What a pall it will cast over the party!"

"Literally!"

"We'll have them running for the door!"

Rosencrantz asked salaciously, "Did you ever bathe in hollandaise?"

"Sounds divine."

"Tonight you'll find out. The egg yolks make it sticky. We'll be holed-up for days licking it off."

Guildenstern rested his head on Rosencrantz's back and said, "I just adore society, don't you?"

$\mathcal{T}$HIRTY

Kevin was red in the face as he shouted, "I don't believe you! All these years you tell me, 'Call it making love! Don't call it fucking! Call it making love.' And now when I say I want to make love, you say you want to fuck!"

Alex was close to tears but shouted back, "Sometimes I want to make love! Sometimes I just want to fuck."

"But when I say fuck you get mad!"

"I never said it made me mad. I said it made me angry."

Kevin threw both his arms wide and screamed, "I'll do whatever you want! Is making love sucking cock? Or is it fucking? Or is fucking fucking?"

Alex whimpered, "Are you making fun of me?"

"Are you trying to make me nuts? Let's make a code for what you want."

Alex narrowed his eyes and glared hatefully at Kevin. "And then last week you called me 'honey'."

Kevin stared back with a blank look on his face. "What? I called you 'honey'? Isn't that good?"

"You know! You know!"

"What? What do I know? You said you wanted me more affectionate. So I called you 'honey'. What are you mad about?"

"You called me 'honey' because you take me for granted. You think I'm just some throw rug you can kick around, some comfortable old overcoat waiting in the closet–"

"You got all that out of my calling you 'honey'?"

"Ricky Ricardo calls Lucy 'honey'. That's for old married couples—"

Kevin interrupted, "What are we?"

Alex finished his thought, "—old married couples who have reached the end of the line. I'm leaving you."

"What?!"

"You always threaten to leave me. But it's me—"

Kevin interrupted again, "You mean 'It's I'—"

Alex shrieked, "I'm the one what's leaving! Goodbye forever!"

$\mathcal{T}$HIRTY-ONE

Dutchman's skin was a dull gray color, and his eyes were listless and red. He was usually hesitant about discussing his will, but today he was anxious to.

On the heels of a bad coughing spell he asked Applegate, "So you're my executrix, right?"

"Executor. Right."

"So you'll make sure that everyone gets what I want them to get?"

"That's my job."

Dutchman coughed violently. "It ain't nothing in there for you."

"I told you, I can't be in the will."

"Because you're my executrix?"

"Because it's against the rules of the clinic."

"But I want to give you something."

"It's not necessary."

Applegate looked around the usually bustling apartment. "Where is everyone?"

"They're gone."

"Gone where?"

"I threw their asses out. I don't want no cackling queens eating my food and drinking my beer and watching my TEE-vee…"

"So you're all alone?"

Dutchman mumbled, "Except at night, when the angels come."

"What? I didn't hear you."

Dutchman was silent a long time. Finally he said, "Make sure Calvin gets the stereo. I promised him the stereo. And I want my sister to have the stone bookends. She's always after me about the damn bookends."

"Don't be so sure you're going to die. You might outlive us all."

Dutchman laughed. "Yeah, I might outlive you all!"

After he left, Applegate checked his pocket. He felt something foreign. He brought it out and looked at it. It was a small, jeweled pin, shaped like a wasp, with red stones for eyes. The wings were delicately painted yellow and green, outlined in gold and encrusted with white stones. The white abdomen was trimmed in gold with more red stones. Applegate had seen Dutchman wearing it at his birthday party and had admired it.

*T*HIRTY-TWO

A week after his personal ad appeared, Applegate called for his responses. There was only one message for him:

"Hi, Jerry, my name is Bob. I saw your ad, and I'd like to talk with you. I'm kind of new at all this. Please give me a call whenever you can."

Applegate delayed for several days. The prospect was exciting but intimidating. Eventually he worked up the nerve to call.

"Hi, I'd like to talk to Bob, please.

"Speaking.

"This is Jerry. From the personals."

"Hi Jerry! I'm glad you got through. I've spent the whole evening helping my son write a term paper."

"Really? You have a son?"

"Yeah, his name is Billy. Twelve years old."

"No kidding. How old does that make you?"

"I'm 35."

"I just turned 30. Does your son live with you?"

"No, with his mother."

"I don't really know where to begin. Is this the first time you've ever answered a personal ad?"

"Yeah."

"That's too bad. This is my first time, too. I guess neither of us knows where to go with this."

Bob said, "Let me start by saying that you won't get any bullshit from me. I'll always tell you what I like and what I don't. I'm up front about my needs. And I'll always be straight with you. If you have any questions, just ask me and I'll give you an honest answer. Honest in keeping with my interpretation of what you really mean."

Applegate laughed. "I'm not sure what that means."

"It means whatever I want it to mean."

"You don't sound new at this."

"I am. I've been married for 14 years. Pretty much isolated all that time. I don't get to the city much."

"Where do you live?"

"Oak Park."

"I grew up near there. In Melrose Park."

"So now that I'm divorced, I'm trying to get around more."

Applegate began to relax. "Sounds very similar to my situation. I'm just in the process of coming out."

Bob was puzzled. "You are?"

"Yeah."

"But your ad said you have your own equipment."

Applegate paused before asking, "Equipment?"

"That's why I was intrigued. I've done some experimenting on my own with enemas, but I was excited by your mention of butterscotch–"

"Bob, I think you answered the wrong ad."

"I did? I thought it was–"

"My ad said nothing about enemas. Or butterscotch. Mine was about coming out issues, going to brunch."

"Well, look, maybe we can still–"

"Thanks, I don't think so." Applegate hung up in a panic.

Applegate thought a long time. The sincere ad had gotten only one response, and that was a mistake. Didn't gay men care about helping another gay man come out? Did they only want sex and money?

Sex and money...

He decided to place another ad. Just as an experiment. He wrote:

GWM, 25 years old, successful attorney, Tom Cruise type, seeks horny men for hot times. Send description of your wildest fantasy.

THIRTY-THREE

Applegate and Elyssia were having absinthe at the Blue Gardenia. Applegate said, "Thanks. You were right. It was a good idea to come here tonight."

Elyssia smiled regally. "Got to get back on the horse that threw you. Speaking of which, is that horse's ass here tonight?"

Applegate had been scanning the bar since they arrived. "No, not here. You know, I really feel bad about Myrtle."

"Myrtle?"

"Or Mabel, or whatever her name was. You know, the queen in Oscar's that I called a whore. I mean, here she was being friendly, and I accuse her of sleeping with Raymond, and then I call her a whore. I wish I could apologize."

"Well, if you see her, say hi and see how she responds."

"Know what ran through my mind when I called her that?"

"What?"

"Well, there's this scene in *La Traviata* where Alfredo calls Violetta a whore, and he throws a purse of money at her feet."

Elyssia whispered confidentially, "He carries a purse? Does *La Traviata* mean *The Transvestite?*"

"No, no, a purse, you know, a little bag. Like men used to carry."

She sat back and envisioned the scene. "It must be stunning on the operatic stage. I bet he has shoes and belt to match. And maybe a little pillbox hat–"

"Actually, he wears one of those huge Hedda Hopper hats with the ostrich plumes. Anyway, he throws it at her feet–"

"His hat?"

"No, his purse, to make the point that the only reason she had an affair with him was for money, not love. So while I was calling Muriel a whore, I thought of throwing a purse of gold at her feet. It seemed like it would make the moment so much more dramatic. Except I didn't have any gold."

"I suppose you could have thrown some loose change."

"Didn't have that either. All I had was a CTA token."

"Not the same effect. So did she take it?"

"Did who take what?"

Elyssia asked frankly, "Did Violetta pick up the purse that La Transvestite threw?"

"No, you don't get it–"

"Hey, money's money. If a man gives you a purse, you should accept it."

"It was a devastating insult to both her and–"

"I wish a man would insult *me* with a purse of gold."

"But she loved him."

"All the more reason to accept his gift."

Applegate said, "I'll be right back; I suddenly have to go to the washroom."

After he left, Elyssia called over the bartender.

"Excuse me, do you know a man who comes here sometimes named Pinkerton? Tall, dark hair, clean-shaven?"

"That bastard! What did he do to you?"

"No, he didn't do anything. I just want to know–"

"I swear, if I catch that psycho in here again–"

"My friend thinks he's in love with Pinkerton."

The bartender was very concerned. "You're friend? The pussycat who likes Weiss beer?"

"Yeah."

"Look, Pinkerton is a thief, a liar, a drunk and probably a murderer. Anyone who gets mixed up with him ends up dead–or worse!"

Applegate was returning. Elyssia handed the bartender a two dollar tip. When Applegate was next to her she said, "I'm ready to go, how about you?"

"Sure."

As they walked out the door, Applegate saw Matthew coming up the cross street. Applegate ducked down and covered his face with his hand.

"What's wrong?"

Applegate gestured towards Matthew, who was entering the Blue Gardenia. "That's him. That's Pinkerton."

After walking a few moments, Elyssia stopped. "Oh dear, I think I left my wallet on the bar. I'll be right back."

"No, don't go in there–"

"I have to. Unless you want to go for me."

"I'll wait here."

Elyssia walked into the Blue Gardenia, marched directly up to Matthew and tapped him on the shoulder. He turned to look at her.

He was taken aback by her–75 years old, silver-gray hair, pristine pearls at her throat and a grandmotherly voice demanding, "I want you to stay away from Jerry Applegate you psycho!"

Matthew looked at her. "Excuse me?"

Elyssia was also surprised by Matthew; he was completely different than what she expected. He had the same general features which Applegate had described, but his eyes were so soft and sincere…

She repeated, "Jerry Applegate! Leave him alone!"

The bar was very loud. "I don't know any Jelly Mapplethorpe. But with a name like that, I bet he's a real fun guy."

"Are you going to stand there and tell me that on March 31st you didn't go up to Applegate standing over by that wall drinking Weiss and ask him what kind of beer–

"Oh, that guy!"

Elyssia said sarcastically, "Yeah, that guy!"

"You know the date?"

"Of course, it was Dutchman's birthday."

"Who's Dutchman?"

Elyssia announced, "None of your damn business, that's who Dutchman is!"

"Applegate? Dutchman? Do you write childrens stories?"

Elyssia found herself being charmed by Matthew. "As a matter of fact, I do write some poetry–" She remembered why she was here. "Applegate is my dearest friend in the world."

"Is he as shy as you?"

"Do you want another shot of tear gas?"

He could barely hear her over the noise of the bar. "Thank you, but I'm not drinking shots."

She held up her handbag and said, "I carry a brick in here! I could smack you with this purse and knock you out!" She added for emphasis, "Just like La Traviata did to Violetta!"

"Oh, are you going to perform for us? Are you from one of those singing telegram companies?"

"And you wouldn't get to keep the gold either!"

Matt looked at the scowl on her face, the purse poised threateningly in the air. Part of him knew she was serious. Part of him thought she couldn't be. He asked, "What would you charge to haunt a house?"

"Lucky for you I have to run–"

"You have someone else to menace?"

Despite herself, Elyssia laughed. She looked at Matthew; she couldn't imagine him threatening Applegate, much less brandishing a switchblade. She felt an urge to put her arms around him and kiss him on the cheek. She had a gut-level feeling that Applegate had screwed up somehow (it wouldn't be the first time!).

Then she remembered what the bartender had said. She threw her shoulders back and declared, "This is your last warning! Keep away from Applegate!"

After she left, Carlyle asked Matthew, "What was that all about?"

Matt took a long sip of his beer and said, very slowly, "Near as I can figure, she's meeting the Dutchman under the apple tree. So if he comes in here tonight, I'm not supposed to buy him any beer."

HIRTY-FOUR

For the next few weeks, Applegate's mailbox was stuffed every day with responses to the "Tom Cruise" ad. Most were in the form of a resume, listing age, height, likes and dislikes. Several included photos. Virtually every one included the line– "I look much younger than I am, and I'm frequently carded in bars."

There were some well thought out letters which actually provided a fantasy, as requested. One was:

> Dear "Tom",
>
> Tom Cruise has always been the sexiest man on the screen for me. More than anything I love his smile. And I'd love to make you smile, too, especially if you look like him. Tell you what, why don't you lean back, take a few deep breaths, turn down the lights and take off all your clothes, one at a time, as you read my fantasy. I'm already nude and oiled. My dick is pulsating just thinking of your sweet dimples and those deep, piercing eyes.
>
> I'm a lowly accountant at a large loop accounting firm. I've been there three years, and one day we hear that we're getting a new executive from another firm, some young, upstart kid, 25 years old, already an executive, smartass cocky bastard who's got the world by the tail. And then I hear this kid–a kid my age, and I'm struggling to justify my existence in this firm–this kid is going to be my boss! I'm

seething with frustration and injustice. I think I'll show this snot-nose little punk who's who.

Then comes the day when you're supposed to join the firm. It's eight o'clock Monday morning, I'm a little hung-over from a wet jockey shorts contest at L.A. Connection, I'm standing in the elevator on the ground floor, and just as the doors are closing, some obnoxious bastard jams his briefcase in so that the doors converge on it with a BANG! and pop open again. The guy gets on. The banging has reinstated my headache, so I glare at this guy. But when I see his face, I stop glaring and am just amazed.

What eyes! What hair! Perfect nose! Brilliant smile! I'm hypnotized. The guy smiles at me and shrugs. Then I get mad. I say, "What the hell is the matter with you? Couldn't you wait for the next elevator?"

He smiles even more and says, "Calm down, Mary, you'll get your panties in a snit."

Now I'm steaming, but I'm a little scared. Why did he call me Mary? Was it just to insult me? Or did he see I'm gay? In a conservative accounting office, you have to be real careful about this sort of thing.

Even worse, did he say that because he could see I was attracted to him? And I was dying! He was wearing a gray suit, beautiful, draping wool hugging each curve, following the line of the thigh, stretching provocatively in the crotch. The shirt under the jacket outlined well-developed pecs. I was upset that the jacket hung over that sweet behind—I was sure those expertly tailored trousers would reveal the outline of a gorgeous ass.

We rode up in silence. I was angry at him, attracted to him, embarrassed that he could tell so easily I was attracted to him, and, on top of everything else, I was enormously turned on by finding myself so attracted to such a jerk.

I started to feel uncomfortable when I noticed him get off at my floor. A weird idea suddenly struck me. I prayed, "Please, God, don't let this asshole be my new boss!" But it was. It was you on the elevator. And when I got to my desk, they introduced you as "Mr. Cruise", my new supervisor.

I studied your face as I blushed. There was a malicious glint in your eye, a glint that said, "I'm gonna run your ass ragged, boy!" But there was also amusement—the amusement of the victor—and even a trace of arousal. I could tell right away you were gloating over having me in your power. You were thinking of the orders you could give me; you couldn't wait to tell me to jump, so that I'd have to ask, "How high?" You were loving every minute of it. And so was I!

Now, I've never considered myself a masochist—not exactly. Although when I was a little boy, and my daddy would yell at me and pull down my pants and bend me over his knee, giving me a few swats on the bare behind with his open hand—well, when he'd do that, you see, it never really hurt that much. He was just trying to scare me, so he never really hit me, but it always made me feel—you know, all kind of warm and tingly, having a man swatting my little rear end, just kind of warming it up, giving it a little pink glow. And sometimes I'd be naughty just to get him to bend me over like that.

And in a lot of relationships, one night stands and longer-term affairs, I tend to take the submissive role. I love to wait on a man; I love to go get my man a beer while he's watching TV or fix dinner while he reads in the study. And in bed I'm a total sex-slave, doing whatever my man asks.

So right away you clicked into my feelings for you. You knew intuitively that you could boss me around and I'd love it. Many times when I was in your office, standing before your desk as you sat back smirking, you would point to something on the floor, a pen or paper clip which you had planted there, and you would ask me to pick it up.

I'd get so mad at your nerve that I blushed crimson, but I always would go and bend over, and then just stand there for an extra second or two, my ass high in the air facing you, with the slit at the back of my sport coat open wide.

It was 10:00 p.m. the Friday before the Labor Day weekend. The place was deserted. I was planning to go home when you buzzed me and ordered me to get into your office, pronto!

Well, I stormed in. I had had it! I wasn't going to tolerate abuse any more—no more yelling at me, no more condescending tones, no more exasperated looks like you were dealing with a spoiled child. I marched into that office ready to tell you off.

You looked up, saw the determined expression on my face, and you smiled. That infuriating, obnoxious, devastatingly sexy smile of yours! The smile that always made me forgive you. But not this time.

Then I saw what was on your desk. Bills. Bills I had sent to clients. I suddenly wasn't so angry anymore. I noticed right away which bills they were.

Now I want you to know I'm not really a thief. But we're under a lot of pressure at this firm, tremendous pressure, to bill the clients. We get rated by how much we bill. And we bill in increments of quarter-hours. So if I spend 2 minutes on the phone with a client, I have to bill him 15 minutes. And sometimes I'll talk to three or four clients in the same 15 minute period and bill 15 minutes to each of them. So I can sometimes charge a lot more time to clients than I'm actually in the office.

Okay, I suppose maybe occasionally I went a little overboard in the billing and charged for time when I wasn't in the office at all. But you have to understand, it's a cut-throat business, a big accounting firm, and I had to do some cheating to get by. And no one ever noticed. At least, no one until you.

You smiled that cocky, knowing, victorious smile and said, "We seem to have a problem here, Rob. Getting a little over-zealous in our billing, are we?"

I hung my head submissively. I mumbled, "Yes."

You quickly and severely snapped, "Yes what?"

"Yes SIR!" I barked back.

"Now, maybe it's not all your fault. But I don't think the senior partners will feel that way when I tell them."

"Are you going to tell them, sir?"

You sat back in your leather easy chair and put your feet on the desk. I automatically stiffened up and stood at attention. My dick was getting hard. It stuck out at a painful angle. Something told me not to adjust it.

"I don't know. I mean, I can understand the temptation. How many of us have never stolen from our employer? How many people walk off with staples and pens and tape dispensers?"

I began to say, "Sure, a lot—" when you cut me off with a scowl on your face. I snapped back to attention.

You said, "But that's no excuse, is it?"

"No SIR!"

"You still have to be punished, don't you?"

There was a smile in your eyes that infuriated me, but at the same time, my dick was now throbbing and hard, pushing against the fabric of my pants, sticking a half-foot out in front of me, held down at an uncomfortable angle. I shifted my weight. "Yes, sir."

"What do you suggest?"

"Anything, sir. Just please don't turn me in, sir."

You smirked and said, "You'd lose your job, wouldn't you?"

"Yes, sir, and I'm sorry now for what I did. I promise that I won't ever do it again. Please, sir, just punish me yourself, right here, right now."

You took your feet off the desk, leaned forward towards me and folded your hands on your desk. "Just what do you suggest, Robert?"

I grimaced and said, "My daddy used to spank me when I was bad."

"How did he do it?"

"Well, first he made me pull down my pants. And then—"

You interrupted, "Pull down your pants!"

"Yes, sir!" I reached down to my black leather belt. I undid it then unbuttoned my trousers. Next was the zipper. I looked up at you. You were staring fixedly on my hands, licking your lips and smiling that infuriating, sexy, victorious smile. I unzipped the zipper and pushed my pants down to my ankles.

I stood there with my pants down, my boxer shorts now in plain view. I still had on my coat and tie. You said, "Take off that jacket."

I did so, slowly, timidly. You barked, "The tie!" I felt a cool breeze on my bare legs as I reached up and undid the knot of my tie. I pulled it through my collar. "Now the shirt."

I started with the bottom button, which was dangling over my dick. My dick, released from the prison of my pants, was bouncing freely. Its mushroom head poked through the fly of my boxer shorts. I made a move to re-insert it, but I thought better of it. I unbuttoned the next-to-last button and continued to work my way up. In a moment, the shirt was off.

Underneath I was wearing a white athletic undershirt, the kind with no arms, just straps that go over the shoulders. I stood there in my underwear, pants down at the floor, dick peeking out. You got up and came across to the front of your desk.

In your hand you held the pointer that you used in meetings. The pointer was about three feet long, a thin metal tube like a car antenna. You sat back on your desk, facing me. You used the pointer to touch my nipples. You outlined them with the cold, rounded tip of the pointer. Then you took the pointer down, along my belly, to the open fly of my boxer shorts. You ran it along the tip of my dick.

At first I felt ticklish and stepped back. The shiny, cold metal sent a shiver through me. You scowled and said, "Stand still!" I snapped to attention and my dick did likewise, now sticking out a good five inches from the fly.

You ran the pointer over the head of my dick. I felt waves of tingling go up my sides, down my tits, across my shoulders. You poked the pointer into my shorts and gently touched my balls. I was on fire. Then you said, "Take off the undershirt." But now your voice was different, softer, velvety, as your own desire heated to a boiling point.

I raised my arms and removed the shirt. You reached out and pulled down my boxer shorts. I panted in anticipation. I was so turned on a drop of cum was already leaking out of the tip of my dick. I was afraid that if you touched me again I would shoot right into your face, gobs and gobs of hot cum showering over your head and shoulders. I was trembling. I didn't think my knees could support me.

But they didn't have to. You got up, grabbed a stiff wooden chair and brought it to where I was. You sat in the chair, reached up and bent me over your knees.

You sat there a while just looking at my bare ass, now poised and waiting. I felt humiliated and vulnerable. And I was dying for any contact at all. Then you did a peculiar thing—you told me to get up.

I did so. I felt like I had done something wrong, like I had displeased you. I was devastated to think that you weren't going to spank me after all. I was almost crying to think that the punishment was over. Then you reached over to the couch, grabbed a small cushion, placed it on your knees and then bent me over again.

The difference was fantastic! The cushion under my belly raised my ass just enough to make it spread, exposing my glory hole. I felt a hundred times more vulnerable, more in your complete control. Plus, I was about to shoot any minute. The cushion would take all the cum, saving your beautiful wool slacks.

And then you began to lecture me on the evils of cheating. You took your open hand and smacked my bare butt. I let out a little yelp as your hand connected skin to skin with my ass. I could tell you didn't intend to really hurt me; the blow made me tingle, made my ass feel alive.

As I lay there, my head to the floor, my ass to the ceiling, I noticed your shoes. You were every inch an executive. Your shoes were black, conservative, and polished to a high gloss. You seemed to read my mind because you said, "See that shine? You better study it, boy, because from now on, you're shining my shoes every morning. If you don't get them to shine like I want, you'll get more of THIS!" and with that, you smacked my ass again.

By the fourth blow, I couldn't restrain myself any more. My

dick rubbing against the cushion exploded into a thunderous orgasm.
It gushed out stream after stream of hot cum. You laughed and turned
me over just in time to grab my dick and milk the last of the cum.

The next few moments were very blurred. Suddenly I was in
your arms, kissing you over and over, reaching for your shirt, removing
your clothes. We made love like I've never made love before. When
you came, I looked deeply into your eyes at the awe and wonder there,
and I knew that I was your slave for life.

"Rob Lowe"

After a few minutes, Applegate caught his breath. He realized that "Rob Lowe" had not included a return address. He checked the envelope. None there, either. He immediately wrote another ad:

"Rob Lowe": It was tempestuous! I had to wash the sheets. Let's do it again real soon. "Tom Cruise"

Would he respond?

$\mathscr{T}$HIRTY-FIVE

Another Saturday night, and Applegate thought he'd try a new bar. From the outside, the Lucky Horseshoe looked like a quaint Irish bar. Applegate had read some articles about a certain bartender, an attractive, intriguing, totally outrageous man who everyone called Sophie.

Applegate stood outside a moment. The facade, as always, was delightful, full of color and precision. He could feel the vibration of a bass line from a current hot hit. He opened the door.

The place was packed. A dancer–young and pink and animated–bounced around the stage and joked with the patrons. A man came up to him and stuck a five dollar bill into his G-string. The dancer bent over from the waist, knees straight, and languidly kissed him. Drinkers at the bar called out encouragement.

Sophie was dispensing beer and epigrams. The peach light seemed to effuse from the walls. The room was not dark; all detail was visible, from the stitching on the dancer's G-string to the numbers on the bill which protruded from the crevice of his prominently posed rear end. Yet it was nowhere near bright. The details all softened and shimmered rather than being etched. Faces were smooth and eyes twinkled.

A free stool opened at a corner of the bar. Applegate sat and ordered a beer. For a while he just observed, ordering more beer and allowing the kaleidoscope to resolve itself at its own pace. Faces smiled, but in no particular direction and at no discernable object. Chests and arms floated by disengaged from the legs and heads which accompanied them. The blur of friendship and good times emanated like the light, surrounding Applegate and including him in the mist. He didn't need to know the men here tonight in order to be one of them.

As time passed and beer acted, individuals began to assert themselves through the mural. A middle-aged man kissed a laughing companion; a young man peeled off his undershirt and swung it over his head. Sophie exchanged dark glances and surreptitious whispers with a muscular jock. Individual conversations could be discerned through the din of music and bar-talk.

Applegate began to wonder about the dancers, about the whole idea of strippers. It didn't seem exploitative or degrading. On the contrary, the strippers appeared to be having as good a time as anyone. Customers would come up to them and place bills in their G-strings and be rewarded with a kiss and hug. As always, Applegate loved to watch men touching each other.

He wondered about the underlying mechanics. Once the money was in the G-string, of course it belonged to the stripper. Or did it? Could the customer complain that the kiss wasn't good enough and demand a refund? Or even worse, could he ask for change?

And what if a customer walked up waving a ten dollar bill, received his kiss, and kept the money? Could he argue that he was merely speculating? That money had never changed hands? Would the stripper be justified in feeling manipulated? Could the customer argue that the stripper should be more careful? Or would all the strippers be too smart to bestow a kiss before the money was safely ensconced next to their skin?

Then he wondered if the dancers compared notes and engaged in cat-fights backstage over who was the most loved. And what would be more important: the number of bills or the denomination of the bills? If a dancer had, say, a single fifty-dollar bill from a single admirer, would that count for more than, say, 10 or 15 singles and fives from a dozen different admirers? The larger bill shows a greater love, but the greater number of smaller bills shows a larger entourage. Or is the sum total of cash all that counts? Or is it different with each dancer?

A customer walked by the stage. The dancer, seeing him out of the corner of his eye, turned and bent down to receive him. The customer, unaware, kept walking towards the bathroom. It suddenly occurred to Applegate just how vulnerable the dancers were.

Then he noticed that most of the men in the bar were as attractive as the dancers. It seemed a bit silly. Why would these men pay for a kiss which they could easily charge for themselves? This was very different than the demeaning atmosphere of the movie *Gypsy*; here it was almost like a mutual joke. Applegate had an image of a customer paying a dancer for a kiss, and then the two of them trading places and the dancer now paying the customer. One might expect to see a lot of old or unattractive men in a place like this, but such was not the case.

Applegate had automatically settled in at the end of the bar which was used by the dancers as they waited to go on. One, very boisterous and loud, came bounding out of the bathroom and all but jumped up on the bar next to Applegate. The young man called out to Sophie, "I haven't had a kiss from you all week!"

Sophie gave him a quick peck on the cheek. "Look at you! Where did you get that hat!? No wonder the Park District banned you from Belmont Rocks!"

Applegate recognized the young man from somewhere. He was pale and skinny and outrageously effeminate. And he was a stripper here. Applegate had read that some men find queens erotic. He didn't, but he was fascinated by the persona.

The young man got carried away talking to Sophie and, with an expansive sweep of his arm, knocked over Applegate's beer. Sophie wiped it up and replaced it while the young man said, "Oh, handsome, I'm so sorry–"

"No problem. The name's Applegate."

He extended a limp wrist and said, "Throckmorton."

Applegate was feeling rather tipsy. "Forget it. Tell you what, would you like to kiss my hand?"

Throckmorton smiled and did so. Applegate asked, "Would you like to kiss anything else?"

"You look real familiar."

"So do you."

Throckmorton went and danced his set. All the dancers were up for 15 minutes then mingled with the customers. As the next dancer began his act and Throckmorton was gathering up his discarded clothes, he smiled at the new dancer and asked, "So what are you supposed to be, the entertainment?"

The new dancer laughed and said, "Fuck you!"

When Throckmorton returned, Applegate asked, "See that guy in the yellow tank top?"

"Bernie? What about him?"

"Well, I've been watching him… You know what I think?"

"What?"

"I think some of these guys take money for sex."

Throckmorton kept a straight face–mostly because he had no idea if Applegate was kidding or if he actually was as naive as he appeared. "Well, I've heard of such things."

"But that guy he's with, I mean, he's even more attractive than… What did you say his name was? Bernie? He's more attractive than Bernie."

"You think so? Bernie won't like that!" He thought to himself, "And I can't wait to tell him!"

"Have you ever done that?"

Throckmorton waved to a former client and ignored Applegate's question.

Then he turned to Applegate and said breathlessly, "See, that song is 11 minutes long. And we only have 15 minutes, so I prefer to have two or three short ones to one long one and half of another like that, know what I mean? I mean, it's arduous. Simply arduous."

"You looked exotic."

"Exotic? Really? Thank you so much. How did you like the simulated orgasm?"

Applegate stammered. "Well, actually... I mean, the crowd loved it."

"But how about you, baby?"

"Well, I thought... I thought it was a little excessive."

Throckmorton mumbled, "Wearing a shirt like that you've got the nerve to talk about excessive?"

"What?"

"Nothing. Here comes the new guy, Daniel." Throckmorton pursed his lips in disdain as his eyes followed Daniel walking along the wall. "High school jock straight off the football field..."

Applegate's eyes lit up. "Oooooo! I like him!"

"But he's so square, so athletic."

"Do you suppose he accepts Visa?"

$\mathcal{T}$HIRTY-SIX

Applegate had been at Dutchman's hospital bed for two or three hours. Dutchman spent most of that time mumbling or raving. He seemed to be experiencing a vivid dream of paradise. There were strongly religious overtones in the various phrases which slipped out amid the tumble of incoherent words. Dutchman was a regular church-goer who always clung to the Baptist faith. Applegate read a book, occasionally dabbing sweat from Dutchman's forehead. Machines pumping medication and nourishment hummed in the background. The hospital sheets were almost preternaturally white.

Applegate looked up and was startled to see that Dutchman's gaze was clear, his expression peaceful. Apparently he was fully conscious. Dutchman reached out slowly and clasped Applegate's hand. Applegate felt a tingling, a sort of electric charge.

Dutchman said, "I saw the angels."

Applegate whispered gently, "Really? That's wonderful."

Dutchman's eyes were bright with fever, but there was something else animating them. A smile of serenity spread within the contortions of pain. "You don't believe me. You think I was dreaming. But I'm telling you, there were angels in this room." Now Dutchman laughed to himself, "No, I don't suppose you could understand. But I got this virus for a purpose. The angel told me. I'm dying for a purpose." He seemed to drift into delirium.

Applegate thought back to his training. Some PWAs maintained that

AIDS was the best thing ever to happen to them; until they faced death, they never examined their lives. Applegate had virtually dismissed this attitude as the rationalization of people in the final stages of a terminal illness. Now, looking at Dutchman, Applegate began to wonder if it were more.

He'd also read of an AIDS sufferer near death who told his friends how he could feel himself evolving into pure light and energy. Again, Applegate assumed that the patient was simply hallucinating. Could it be real?

Suddenly Applegate thought to himself, "I wonder if Dutchman is scattering?"

Scattering. That was the term which Applegate used to describe the coping mechanisms he had come up with when he was a child being abused by his father. Dr. Bellman referred to it as "dissociative disorder" and "multiple personalities". It was the separation which occurred when the mind was at its limit of pain—the ways in which the mind left the body when faced with horror or anguish which was beyond its threshold.

Once, when Applegate was in a workshop for adult survivors of child sexual abuse, the facilitator asked the group, "How many of you experienced flying around the room when you were being abused?" All 25 men and women raised their hands. It was the most common form of scattering. Multiple personalities was perhaps the most extreme. Applegate had experienced a half-way form of personality split in which he would fly around the room while a second little boy was left behind to face the abuse. Other little boys, with various names and of various ages, had appeared over the years when Applegate needed them to stand in for him. Some still lingered in the background to this day.

Some were not boys at all. Applegate's fascination with Madama Butterfly was borderline scattering. On the three occasions when he'd attempted suicide, the music had been in his head urging him to proceed, whispering to him that peace and fulfillment and infinite rapture were as close as the medicine cabinet or the window.

Scattering was brought about by horror, yet the process itself was beautiful to experience. It seemed to be accompanied by mirrors and prisms and bursts of light. On one particularly gruesome afternoon when Applegate's father had worked himself into a frenzy and pounced on him, Applegate had not merely floated to the ceiling... he'd shot through the roof, losing all contact with his body. Usually he would stay within sight of those two awful, screaming people down below. This time he found himself looking down on the peaceful treetops, grateful for the sudden quiet. When he thought back to that day, Applegate had a vivid image of a beam of light hitting a prism and diffracting into vast rainbows reflected in an infinity of mirrors.

So even the horrors of child rape had their compensations. In his attempt to destroy Applegate's self-esteem, Applegate's father had inadvertently pushed him into a new dimension, a metaphysical reality which Applegate would never have found otherwise.

Reality? If a tree falls in the forest and no one hears it… If Dutchman dies in the hospital and no one cares… If little boys can hover by the ceiling…

And wasn't that the core of Applegate's obsession with Billie Holiday? Hadn't she, also, been forced to construct her own alternate reality? This was different from being driven insane; insanity is generally self-destructive. Scattering had saved Applegate's life, allowing him to survive the abuse at a time when survival itself was in doubt… to bury the horror until he was mature enough and strong enough to deal with it.

And yet wasn't all this contrary to Applegate's message to his migraine clients as well as his own battle with migraines? Scattering is a way of avoiding pain. Applegate always told his clients they must face pain. He never witnessed the scattering effect in his migraine patients, and yet they would emanate a beauty just like Dutchman was now. The same beauty brought about in one case by avoiding pain and in the other by wrestling with it.

Which was Dutchman doing right now? Was this delirium? Or was Dutchman facing a reality which was still outside of Applegate's experience?

Applegate looked up as he felt Dutchman tighten his grip on his hand. Dutchman smiled and whispered, "I think it's time."

"Don't die, Dutchman."

"But the angel is calling to me. Don't you see him? He says I'm ready."

"I'm not ready."

"I'm going now, honey. I'll see you on the other side. I'll be waiting for you."

THIRTY-SEVEN

"How do you like this outfit on me?"

Applegate felt confident after 19 sessions with Chardonnay. He believed he finally knew how to get past her opening gambit. "Very nice. Very nice indeed. Those colors look wonderful on you; avocado highlights your complexion."

Chardonnay basked a moment and asked, "Really? Avocado looks good on me?"

"Wonderful." Applegate began to relax. He was sure the preliminary round would go quickly, and they could actually get some work done.

"And the maroon shoes? They go well with the avocado ensemble?"

"Yes, very nice. You really know how to pick colors that bring out your eyes. Now can we–"

"So these colors are better than, say, orange or tan?"

DANGER! DANGER! DANGER! "Orange and tan? Very nice. Last week I asked you–"

"But when I was wearing orange and tan that time, you said I looked fabulous."

"I don't remember, but–"

"I remember! So what is it?"

"What is what?"

"What brings out my eyes better? Orange and tan? Or avocado and maroon?"

Applegate was desperate. He said, "Have you lost weight?"

"Are you kidding? I'm so fat nothing fits. This is a new outfit."

"It makes you look thin."

"Really?"

"Really."

She said, "I registered for classes last week. I chose to take English Composition."

"That should be interesting."

"No, I hate it."

"Then why did you choose it?"

"You're required to choose it. And Eric still wants his sixty dollars. He's such a nag. He just won't let a dead horse rest."

"Did you try discussing it with him?"

"Yeah, but the talk wasn't fruitworthy. Plus I'm experiencing a negative cash flow position."

"What does that mean?"

"I'm broke."

"I see."

"Sixty dollars would be a hard blow to swallow."

"No doubt."

"Especially since I'm moving right now, and there's a lot of expenses. Do you know about spackle?"

Applegate asked, "Is that some sort of plaster or concrete?"

"That's what I need to find out. I've got to patch some holes in my wall in order to get my security deposit back."

"What kind of holes?"

"Fists."

"Fists? You pound your fists through your walls?"

Chardonnay was incensed. "No! Of course not! What kind of nut do you think I am?"

Applegate restrained himself.

"No, it's my friends. They put their fists through my walls."

"Why?"

Chardonnay looked bewildered. "For some reason, I know a lot of frustrated people. My friends are real characters. I've often thought of writing my autobiography. My life would make a great novel. If not a made-for-TV movie."

"I think you mean in addition to a made-for-TV movie."

"That's what I said. There have been a lot of cliff-dwelling moments. Like the time my new boyfriend accused me of cheating on him."

Applegate wondered to himself, "Cliff-dwelling? Maybe she means cliff-hanging?" He asked her, "Why did he accuse you?"

"Because he caught me at it. Anyway, I talked to my mother again about my quitting dental hygiene school. She's done a three-hundred-sixty degree turn on it."

"You mean she's back where she started?"

"No, just the opposite."

"Then you mean a one-hundred-eighty degree turn. Three-hundred-sixty degrees is full circle."

"Well, not in my mother's case. She's always been perpendicular to my wishes."

Applegate thought a moment and said, "The dealer passes."

"Huh?"

"I said go on."

THIRTY-EIGHT

The responses to the "Tom Cruise" ad continued to arrive:

> The tines of the wire whip bang and clang against the sides of the bowl. I pour on more sugar; the crystals are softly subsumed into the voluptuous yellow cream. I watch them dissolve and then renew my beating with a fervent fury.
>
> How dare you say you'll be late?!
>
> I watch as the whip forms tow lines throughout the egg yolks. I've beaten in a half cup of sugar by now, and the yolks are thick and pale yellow. I continue to whip with such intensity that I fear I will chip the bowl.
>
> "An emergency." (What a transparent lie!) "An emergency came up." (I bet something came up...)
>
> I raise the whip from the bowl. The thick cream forms a ribbon, cascading down into the yolks, holding its form a moment before gently melting into its source. I dip in a finger, penetrating the satiny sheen. I am enveloped by liquid velvet. I raise the custard to my lips. I take a hesitant nip and then draw my finger across my tongue, lapping up the rich, sweet cream, allowing thick, sticky drops to fall down my chin onto my apron, sucking and slurping in an oral ecstasy. I've

added Grand Marnier to give it a slight orange taste and a touch of
Wild Turkey for an added kick. If this dessert doesn't get you into my
bed (when you finally deign to show up), nothing will.

I turn my attention to the egg whites. They sit in the bowl,
unbeaten, an undefined mass of raw protein. They slip and slide inside
the bowl, making slight smacking sounds. I take my fresh wire
whip–not the one which I've used for the yolks, because any trace of
yolk will deflate the whites–and, with my pristine new whip, begin to
slog my way through the sticky, warm gelatinous mush.

A drop of white lands on my hand. I stop beating a moment.
I smear the egg white into my skin. As I take my finger away, a tiny,
gossamer strand of egg white stretches between my hand and finger.
So much like cum, like your warm, sticky cum on my face. I envision
the streams of hot cum shooting out of you, warm and frothy.

I resume whipping the whites. The quivering mass begins to
take on form and color. As I beat more and more air into them, they
turn a frosty, pale white. They attain shape and substance.

Now the bowl is filled to the brim with stiff, satiny meringue.
I take the whip from the bowl; it leaves behind a mound of egg white,
soft, shiny and firm. It is shaped like a woman's breast. It even has a
point at the top, like a firm, erect nipple. I think about the story I
heard… that champagne glasses were originally fashioned in the shape
of one of Marie Antoinette's breasts.

I bend forward, extending my tongue to give the meringue
breast a sloppy kiss. As I stand back up, I see a dollop of meringue on
the tip of my nose. My tongue expertly licks it off.

As I fold the meringue into the custard and add the orange
juice-gelatine mixture, you ring my bell.

"Well, it's ABOUT TIME!" I screech.

The look on your face says you are not in the mood for this
tone. Too bad. That's the tone of the evening.

You say, "Oh, baby, I'm so sorry–"

But I cut you off. I scream and sputter, "I spend all day slav-
ing over a hot stove to make you a feast! Medallions of veal with
bechamel sauce! Asparagus dripping with butter! Crisp celery hearts
with olive oil and lemon! Everything warm, moist, dripping, oozing
with cream and oil, all attending your pleasure, every morsel created
with you in mind–"

"Bitch!" You kiss me hard on the lips. I slap you.

You're angry now. You reach out and grab the boat of ched-
dar cheese sauce. You grab the waistband of my jeans, pull it forward,

and pour the sauce in.

I feel the thick, warm sauce fill my shorts, spread over my thighs, under my balls, along my shaft, forming a pool at the end of my cock where it's trapped by my jockey shorts. When I go to move, I make a slushing noise.

Incensed, I pick up a wedge of sliced avocado, seasoned with thyme and basil and swimming in olive oil, and squish the soft flesh into your forehead. The green chunks cascade down your face, the fat in the avocado leaving shiny trails on your cheeks.

You rip off my shirt. You grab at my jeans, unbuttoning them, pulling them roughly down. You reach for my shorts next, pulling them along my legs, sticky with cheese sauce. Within a moment I'm nude before you. You take the cruet of olive oil and douse me with it, rubbing it into my hair, massaging it across my chest, pouring it into the crack of my ass where I feel it ooze into my asshole and cling to the little hairs.

Now I tear at your clothes. We both begin to shout obsceni-ties at each other: Bitch! Whore! Asshole! Fuck you! Eat my cum! Fuck fuck fuck! When we are both naked, I rush to the orange mousse on the counter, now firm and warm. I shove my hand deep into it. I feel the cream and custard and frothy egg whites, and thrill in the rush of orange scent released by my disturbing the mixture: a scent of Grand Marnier and Wild Turkey, the voluptuous cream, the eggs and sugar, all of it now firm from the gelatin, quivering with my hand buried deep in the mold.

You see me. You know that I'm about to throw a handful of mousse at you. You rush towards me. In a panic I pick up the entire mold and hold it over my head. Just before you reach me I hurl the contents at you. We are both caught in an explosion of orange mousse.

You grab me around the waist. We fall in each other's arms, clawing, scratching, biting, shouting. We struggle across the floor, slithering and sliding in an orange slick, my hands in your ass, your lips on my right nipple, my mouth to your ear, your hands on my balls. Everywhere is orange and egg and mounds of satiny, stiff souffle. I hear you growl like a lion; I snarl back. I feel a new warmth, a new cream between us. The cream hits my belly and slides down my thigh, as I hiss and scratch and feel my own cream now mix with yours. Awash in avocado and oil and mousse, we lay in each other's arms, panting.

Alex

161

"Alex"? The return address seemed very familiar.

There was another response, peppered with misspellings and spasmodic punctuation, perhaps the most bizarre of all:

1. *Why do you want to join the Order?*
2. *How did you hear about it?*
3. *Do you know anyone else whose in the Order*
4. *How long have you known Clarissa*
5. *Have you and Clarissa ever had misunderstandings - (example) Were they resolved?*
6. *If Clarissa decided to become active or if she cannot make most of the meetings would that affect you in any way*
7. *How much free tome to you have*
8. *How would you be able to help the order*
9. *Are you a scary person?*
10. *List some of you're fears?*
11. *How old are your children*
12. *Do you have access to a vehicle*
13. *Are you a patient person?*
14. *What are some of the things you've heard about the Order*
15. *Bring goat food*

Applegate came across a letter with a Louisiana postmark. The handwriting was childish and unsteady. He opened it and read:

Dear ????,

Hi my name is Sandy. I don't know yurs. I saw your add in a mag my friend gave me and I thought I'd write. don't have a lot of friend and can we be frineds? I'm pretty lonely write now. Is that to much to ask? All I want is a person to write to.

I don't get a lot of mail from my family. That is why I am writing hoping I can find someone to write Back and forth to. I hope you are an understanding person? I used to live in Kentucky, that is were I was born and raised. I had a lover there who was very abusive and hit me all the time. I loved him more than anything in the world. But one time he come home drunk and beat me. I called my friend Billie and she picked me up and we went to Louisiana. We met a guy who said he'd give me a job and we became lovers but then he tried to rape me and I killed him. I did not mean to but he was hurting me and the gun went off and they gave me 20 years.

I been locked up for five years. In that time I been raped four times. The warden and the guards they will not do nothing to help me because I am GAY and as far as they are concerned it is the Gay man who is always at fault and scum. They treat me like shit because of my gay and they don't do nothing to protect me. And I don't have no one to write to and no one to write back. Nobody sent me a card on my birthday last year.

When they find out I in prison they never write back and I don't understand why? All I want is someone to keep in touch with. Is that too much to ask? Am I wrong for trying to find a friend?

Well I better go and hope with what little hope I have left that you will at least write a letter and at least let me know your name. But I hope we can become close pen pals??????

Thank you for your time?????

Yours truly,
Sandy

It caused Applegate some dismay. Certainly he could not ignore such a pathetic plea for help, but Sandy was in prison for murder. Did Applegate want to get involved with such a person?

A twenty-year sentence. When would he be up for parole? Applegate would feel a lot better about writing if he knew that Sandy wouldn't be out of jail for many years.

Oh, what the hell! Applegate picked up a yellow note-pad and began, "Dear Sandy..."

$\mathcal{T}$HIRTY-NINE

Elyssia's death was painful but not devastating. It seemed like a natural part of the grand cycle: she was 75, had lived a full life, and died in the natural order of things. Dutchman's death had been an obscene aberration.

Forty

As he dragged a gnat carcass across the shelf, Rosencrantz noticed Guildenstern finally waking up. "Well, it's about time, sleepyhead!"

Guildenstern held his head in four hands and moaned, "Ohhhhh, I think I'm sick…"

"I'm not surprised. You polished off at least a tablespoon of whiskey last night."

"Was it that much?"

"You really made a pig of yourself."

"I couldn't help it. Empty bottles, pizza crusts…"

"Those guys over in 312 sure know how to party."

After the humans in 312 had passed out, a few dozens of the building's roaches had held their own little party.

Rosencrantz thought back to last night, "Remember when Gordy was waltzing on the face of that guy snoring on the floor!"

Guildenstern took his hands away from his face and laughed. The laugh was cut short by a gasp of pain, but he smiled as he said, "And then the guy suddenly breathes in unexpectedly!"

"I'll never forget that look on Gordy's face as he went under!"

"For a brief moment, a crunching sound, and then snoring again like nothing happened!"

"I bet he had a funny taste in his mouth when he woke up!"

Guildenstern chortled evilly, "I wonder if he swallowed Gordy whole or if he was spitting up a leg or two this morning!"

Rosencrantz asked in a deceptively casual tone, "Do you remember flirting with Mack?"

"I wasn't flirting with Mack! He was flirting with me. And you didn't have to bite his head off."

Rosencrantz smiled smugly. "You mean when I used my rapier wit to reduce him to tears!? He didn't stand a chance. I was in top form! Remember how he tried to do a Charles Bronson impression and I asked if he was doing Wayne Newton!? He was so mad he was sputtering!"

"No, I was talking about after all that, when you opened your ponderous and marble jaws and bit his head off."

"Oh. Well… I suppose that was a tad anticlimactic after the verbal trouncing I gave him."

"What else happened last night? Did I do anything unspeakable?"

Rosencrantz asked, "You don't remember the dance?"

Guildenstern curled up and buried his head in eight hands, pleading, "Not the mambo! I didn't do the mambo!"

"*Au contraire!*"

"Oh God. Is there any more?"

"As a matter of fact, you wore an accoutrement! You took tiny bits of fruit and put them on your head and told everyone you were Carmen Miranda!"

"No! Please! Tell me it ain't so!"

"EVERYBODY MAMBO!"

In order to think of anything but Carmen Miranda, Guildenstern asked, "What are you doing with that gnat?"

Rosencrantz took on his lecture-tone, but kept it gentle because Guildenstern was so hung-over. "It's time you realized that being a cockroach isn't all glamour and glitz. It's a business, with gruntwork and details and a thousand little pains in the ass. See this gnat?"

"Yes."

"When Applegate gets home in an hour, he's going to have his glass of iced tea as usual. But when he goes to take that first sip, he's going to find this gnat floating on the top. Or maybe just after he takes his first sip. And how do you think it's going to get there?"

Guildenstern asked hesitantly, "You're going to plant it in his glass?"

"No, *we're* going to plant it there."

"I'm sorry if I haven't been doing my share. I'm kind of new to this."

"Being a cockroach is a never-ending job. It's the little touches that mean so much. A gnat in your iced tea might not seem like much, and it's sure a lot of work and effort and time, but it's all worth it when you see Applegate's face light up! All the heartache and sleepless nights pay off when I can make his eyes open like they do!"

Guildenstern said dreamily, "Know what I like the best?"

"What?"

"It's when he walks in the room, sits down, starts reading or working on his computer or whatever, and like ten minutes later he looks up and spots me. You know, when he suddenly realizes that I've been there all along, in plain sight, and he hasn't noticed me."

"And that's difficult with someone like Applegate. He can really spot a roach. He can see roaches that aren't even there."

"A good trick."

"That's what we're here for–to show him the difference between real roaches and phantom roaches. My favorite is the staccato scream, the 'Ah! Ah! Ah! Ah! Ah! Ah! Ah! Ah!', all in rapid-fire succession like a jackhammer or a machine gun." Rosencrantz thought a minute and continued, "I'm going to miss him when we leave."

"Don't worry, darling. There are millions of people in the naked city, and each one has their own unique scream just waiting to be used on us."

ORTY-ONE

Applegate walked up to the apartment building. There was an older man in the front yard, looking very concerned. With a thick accent he asked Applegate, "How we get in?"

Applegate said, "Well, I suppose we just ring." He found Vogel's name and rang the buzzer. There was no response. Then he noticed a sign, written on a paper plate and taped to the main door, announcing "Our buzzers aren't working. Please yell to the upper right window."

Applegate looked up. The window above him to the right was open. He thought a moment, looked around, and finally yelled, "Hello?" The old man was staring at him in amazement. Applegate yelled again, "Is anybody there?" No response.

Several moments passed. Then Applegate heard a sound. Another old man, looking very similar to the one in the front yard with Applegate, came out the main door and gestured to the first man. Applegate nodded and walked past him into the hallway. He found apartment 2C and knocked.

No response. He knocked again. A very suspicious voice asked, "Who's there?"

"My name is Jerry Applegate. From Wilson Clinic." No response. "We have a lunch date. Your buzzer is broken."

Vogel opened the door angrily. "No it's not. That sign doesn't mean anything."

What struck Applegate first was the smell of the room. It was like a zoo. He walked into the tiny apartment; the main room was almost overwhelmed by the twin bed in the middle. Against every wall were cages, terrariums and aquariums.

Vogel looked at Applegate and said very curtly, "I'm on the phone." He walked off to a small side-room and left Applegate standing alone.

It was the first week in August and hot enough to make the atmosphere in the room stifling. A large black-and-white cat lay on the unmade bed. Applegate extended two fingers for it to sniff. It did so. Having established a relationship, Applegate began to rub it behind the ears. It nuzzled against his fingers. Suddenly there was rapid movement on the floor. Applegate was frightened, but then realized it was a kitten. The kitten began to climb up the side of the bed. It had the typical crazy-eyed look of all kittens when they get excited, and it moved in hyper-kitten fashion up the blanket, across the bed and head-over-heels down the opposite side. Applegate laughed.

The smell of animal was overwhelming. The largest cage was occupied by a rabbit and a gerbil. There were at least a dozen birds in another. Two small terrariums sat in front of the single window in the room. Applegate bent over them. He just about fell over backwards when he saw a tarantula in one. He didn't want to know what was in the other.

Several terrariums along the floor appeared to hold dozens of mice. Some larger, furry creatures with red eyes were kicking up wood chips in a low, squat cage.

Finally Vogel returned. "I've been on hold all this time! The motherfuckers!"

"On hold?"

"That's what I said!" Vogel was consumed with rage. "I'm not ready yet. You'll just have to wait!"

"That's okay. I've been making the acquaintance of your cat and kitten."

Vogel seemed to loosen up just a little. He said, with a half-smile, "Two kittens. See?" He pointed to two almost identical kittens wrestling in the corner.

"Oh, I didn't see the other one."

"Their mother is dead."

"That's too bad."

Vogel's anger returned in full force. "They killed her! The dirty bastards!"

"Who killed her?"

"My fucking neighbors. They had her destroyed."

"That's terrible."

"She got out! Just once! One time she got out of the apartment and they killed her! They all knew she was my cat! See that?" Vogel pointed out the window to a green sign on the fence. "That's where they put the posters. Where they knew I couldn't see them. Facing away from my apartment! How was I supposed to see the posters when they deliberately had them facing away from me?"

"Who put up posters? The people who found your cat?"

"Don't take their side! They just wanted the shelter to kill her. They couldn't wait. The lousy motherfuckers!"

Applegate felt he was in beyond his depth. Vogel was more than depressed; he appeared to be paranoid. Apparently some well-meaning neighbors had found his cat, brought it to the animal shelter, and even placed signs in the area announcing that fact; yet Vogel had managed to twist it into a plot against him personally. Perhaps this was AIDS dementia. Perhaps the clinic had made a mistake assigning Applegate to Vogel.

"Wait here. I'm going to take a shower." Vogel went into the bathroom. Applegate made scratching sounds on the blanket with his fingernails. The kittens responded immediately, charging up the sides of the bed, tumbling over one another, jumping a foot into the air and falling over the side.

When Vogel returned several minutes later he said, "I have to feed the pythons before we go."

"Pythons?"

Looking at Applegate as though he were unbelievably stupid, Vogel said, "What do you think the mice are for?"

In the far corner was a terrarium with a single branch. Applegate now noticed two snakes less than a foot long each. Vogel said, "See, baby pythons."

"And they eat mice?"

"Baby mice." Vogel had placed one of the mouse cages on the bed and was reaching in. Applegate jumped back when he saw what appeared to be a nest of cockroaches. Then he realized they were baby mice no bigger than bugs.

Vogel grabbed two. He went over to the snake terrarium and took off the lid. "Want to watch?"

"Sure."

Vogel held one tiny baby mouse by the tail, dangling it in front of a snake. It struck at the mouse, almost too quick to see. Then it sat back with the fat little baby mouse sticking out of its wide-open mouth. Vogel repeated the procedure with the second snake.

Applegate asked, "They're not poisonous, are they?"

"No, they're constrictors. They've struck at my fingers, but they've never broken the skin. They prefer to squeeeeeeze their enemies to death." The image obviously delighted Vogel.

Vogel and Applegate left. When they reached the front door Vogel angrily ripped down the paper-plate sign. "There is nothing wrong with my buzzer!" he insisted as he crumpled it up and threw it on the lawn.

His mood was not improved by a stroll down Halsted Street. "Look at that! Twenty-five dollars for a shirt. Is that robbery? Is that fair? How do they expect people to spend that kind of money?"

Applegate said, "Well, actually, it's a nice shirt—"

"Not for twenty-five dollars!"

Vogel wanted to grab a hamburger at the little stand on the corner. As they sat at the outdoor table, he said, "Look at that old man wearing tight jeans like that. He looks like hell. Doesn't he know what he– DAMN! DAMN!"

Vogel's outburst startled Applegate. "What's wrong?"

Vogel looked wild-eyed at Applegate. "Didn't you hear me? Didn't you hear me tell that guy NO LETTUCE?"

"Actually, I wasn't listening."

"I did! I'm not a fucking rabbit!" He stormed off to complain. He returned a few minutes later, still as angry.

Applegate said, "I've been a friend-in-need for about a year now. I understand you had another friend-in-need a few months back."

Vogel said very curtly, "She hasn't called."

"That's what my supervisor told me. I read your file, but those files tend to be out of date and disorganized. Have you ever been hospitalized?"

"No. Not for AIDS."

"You never had any infections?"

"I had severe ARC. Back when they called it ARC. What do they call it now?"

"I think they say HIV positive symptomatic."

"And that's supposed to make it easier?"

Vogel's indefatigable bitterness was overwhelming Applegate. He began to sincerely doubt that he could help Vogel. Vogel's problems were perhaps too severe, and Applegate was not a psychologist.

Vogel suddenly said, "I saw my buddy Evan the other day."

"How was that?"

"You know what that bastard did?"

"Tell me."

"See, we had sex twice altogether. Me and Evan had sex twice. Evan and Serge, my other friend, have had sex together four times. So the other day, when I saw Evan, I told him I was horny. And out of nowhere he says he's not in the mood. Can you imagine?"

"Well, that happens."

Vogel sprang forward in his chair, clenched his fists and snarled, "GOD... DAMN... IT! He was teasing me. That's all he was doing, he was playing games. I told him he was going to regret it when we got outside, and he did."

Applegate began to feel the phantom cockroaches crawling under his shirt. Vogel's eyes were wild, his mouth drawn and ugly. Applegate didn't know if he could deal with what Vogel was about to say, but he asked anyway, "What... what do you mean?"

"I beat the crap out of him. He had it coming."

Applegate shifted uncomfortably in his chair, swatting at his chest. "You beat him up?"

"He was sorry he said no to me. He won't say no again." Applegate stared at him. Vogel announced defiantly, "He had it coming. Didn't he? Well, didn't he?"

Applegate tried to remain calm. He tried to resist the urge to run from Vogel as fast as he could. He reached down to the keychain canister of tear gas and removed the safety. He said, "Well, he has the right to say no–"

Vogel pounded the table. "But don't you see? He slept with Serge four times. And only twice with me."

"You and Serge are separate persons–"

Vogel looked as though he would leap from his chair. "No we're not! Sexually we're not! Sexually we're identical! Same hair, same body, same technique! Sexually we're identical! He had no right to have sex with him and not me!"

Anger, Applegate could deal with. Rage, bitterness, pain, death, loneliness, he could deal with. But sexual violence? No, it was too much. He thought of the beatings he had endured when he tried to resist the sexual advances of his own father–beatings which ended in rape anyway, so nothing was gained by his resistance.

Nothing gained? By his attempt to assert his humanity? Applegate thought back to those terrible years. When he had resisted his father, he hadn't won. He hadn't been able to escape the abuse… but even the attempt to defend himself, even the very realization itself that he had the right to resist… Didn't that count for something?

Nothing gained?

He looked at Vogel. Applegate was startled to see Dutchman's eyes staring back at him. The same eyes as at their first meeting that day when Applegate walked into the hospital room. Dutchman was lying amid the white sheets and pillows; the bed seemed enormous, it seemed to swallow up Dutchman's tiny, emaciated body. The only thing about Dutchman that was alive and vibrant were his eyes… vibrant with terror and pain, alive with confusion and despair.

Yet somehow Dutchman had overcome it. Even in death he had made a stand. Even through PCP and a hundred infections, through herpes and rashes and diarrhea, he had asserted his dignity; he had declared himself a human being. And somehow that declaration alone had won him something. Somehow he had triumphed, in some obscure, undefinable, totally irrational manner.

Nothing gained?

And now Dutchman's eyes were staring out of Vogel's face. All eyes are the same when they look at death. Applegate saw Dutchman. He saw Vogel. He saw an hysterical 10-year-old boy trying to resist the sexual advances of his own father.

Applegate's voice was gentle and firm. "Yes, Vogel, I think we'll work well together. I'd like to meet with you once a week. Would that be alright?"

Vogel spoke with fierce resentment. "Once a week? You think I have nothing better to do with my time?" The anger in his voice was contradicted by the pleading in his eyes.

Applegate said, "I know it's a lot of time, but I think we could help each other."

In a bitchy tone Vogel decreed, "Well, it can't be Thursday. I go to the hospital on Thursday."

"That's fine with me."

"And it can't be Tuesday either." He smacked his open hand on the table as he shouted, "Do you hear me? It can't be Tuesday."

"I understand. How about Wednesday?"

Vogel seemed younger and more scared. Dutchman's eyes glimmered with hope... and smoldered with terror. "Yeah, Wednesday. But not too early. I don't get up until noon."

"I'll be by Wednesday at 1:00. That will be our time, okay?"

Vogel didn't have the energy to maintain his anger anymore. His voice trembled as he asked, "You won't stand me up?"

"No, I promise I'll be there."

With superhuman effort Vogel replaced the mask. "You'd better be. If you don't show, I'll come after you. I'll hurt you." He was suddenly seized with a fit of violent coughing.

Applegate looked at the pale, skinny, young man threatening him, the slight frame which looked as though it might not survive the coughing fit. He replaced the safety on his tear gas and returned the canister to his pocket. "Don't worry. I'll be there."

FORTY-TWO

Throckmorton asked Applegate, "Are you going to the Halsted Street Fair this weekend?"

"Sure, I'm looking forward to it."

"Would you like to meet me and some friends there?"

"Sounds nice."

"Good. There's one friend in particular I think would like to see you again." Since getting to know Applegate, Throckmorton had been feeling a bit guilty for all the times in the Blue Gardenia when he had tried to discourage Matthew from approaching him—not to mention the times he had referred to Applegate as "weirdo over there" and "the silent sicko." "How about 8 o'clock, Saturday night?"

"I'll be there."

Throckmorton added, "At the Blue Gardenia."

Applegate hesitated a moment before repeating, "Oh, the Blue Gardenia?"

"Sure, I've seen you there lots of times."

"Well, not for a while now. It's kind of a rough place."

"Rough?" Throckmorton looked over his shoulder confidentially and fluttered his hands. "Well, I did hear some gossip that a few weeks ago this queen threw acid in some faggot's face and blinded him, and the faggot knifed the queen to death. But I think it's probably an exaggeration."

Applegate reflected a moment. "What the hell. He probably won't be anywhere near the Blue Gardenia."

"Who won't?"

"Oh, this guy I'm avoiding. With all the gay bars in Chicago, the chances are a thousand to one that he'll just happen to be in the Blue Gardenia... at 8:00... this Saturday."

The next day, Throckmorton called an old friend. "Matthew? It's Throckmorton. Calling to remind you about Saturday night."

"8 o'clock, the Blue Gardenia. I'll be there."

No sooner had Throckmorton hung up than the phone rang again. "Hello?"

"Hi Throckmorton. This is Pinkerton."

"Pinkerton! Where have you been for the last few weeks? Alcatraz?"

"Very funny."

"I haven't seen you around so I just assumed–"

"I got in a little trouble, and I was just laying low."

"Speaking of laying–and low is my favorite way–how's your love life?"

"Congratulate me! I've got myself a new husband. I think this is the real thing. The man I've been waiting for."

Throckmorton wedged the phone on his shoulder and filed his nails as he said, "I see."

"But I thought this weekend might be a good time for us to get out, circulate a little, meet some old friends. If there's going to be commitment and understanding, if our relationship is to grow and develop–"

Throckmorton was applying cold cream to his face as he interrupted, "You two are sick to death of each other."

"If I spend one more night alone with this asshole, I swear I'll shoot myself. It was great while his lover was alive. Calvin just saw me on the side now and then. After Dutchman died–"

"Dutchman?"

"Calvin's lover. After he died, Calvin moved in with me. And I'm ready to jump out the window."

"You could tell him it's over."

"Not Calvin. He just won't let go. He's a regular Ivana Trump."

"You can make him let go."

"You don't understand."

"I think I do. And I hope I don't hear about Calvin turning up dead."

Pinkerton laughed a hollow laugh. "Dead! That's funny. Calvin dead. Funny. Anyway, the fair is this weekend. Where's everyone going to be?"

"Saturday night, 8 o'clock, the Blue Gardenia. They will let you in the Blue Gardenia, won't they?"

"Well, if I wear a hat and keep my collar up."

"You didn't really steal Matthew's wallet, did you?"

"Throckmorton! I'm shocked at you!"

"Do you still have it? There was a business card he wanted from it."

"No, I threw it out. Bastard only had twenty dollars, so what's he crying about?"

"Matt can be so inconsiderate. But far be it from me to turn in a sister. Your secret is mine. See you Saturday. Will you bring Calvin?"

"Are you kidding? Of course. That shit-head is terrified of being alone. Scared of ghosts. There's only one thing he's more scared of than being alone."

"What's that?"

"Cockroaches. He's got the worst roach-phobia I've ever seen."

Throckmorton asked, "Really? Worse than yours?"

Pinkerton laughed. "Well, almost…"

In an elegant hotel, Jacques Hardoné combed his hair and contemplated his divine face. The phone rang.

It was Anna, his screenwriter. "Jacques? What's the schedule?"

"We're almost done shooting. Should wrap it up tomorrow."

"When do we go back to LA?"

"Not till Monday. Whenever I'm in Chicago in the summer, I try to check out the Halsted Street Fair. In fact, what are you doing Saturday? Want to go with me?"

"Sure, why not?"

"Tell you what, meet me there. Do you know where the Vortex is?"

"Can't say I do."

"How about Sidetrack?"

"Don't know that either."

Jacques said, "I know. The Blue Gardenia. It's right on the corner of Halsted and Melrose."

"I suppose I can find that."

"Meet me there about 7:00, okay?"

"Sure."

"Wait. Anna?"

"Yes?"

"Better make that 8:00."

Rosencrantz said to Guildenstern, "Let's go apartment hunting."

"Sounds divine."

"Saturday night, Applegate is going to the Halsted Street Fair. We'll hitch a ride on his cuffs. It will be a good opportunity to meet prospective hosts."

$\mathcal{F}$ORTY-THREE

At 8:00 o'clock on Saturday evening, Halsted Street was packed. Traffic was closed off, and along both curbs were hundreds of vendors selling hand-made jewelry, x-rated videos, macrame plant hangers, sex toys, off-beat underwear, handpainted ties, rocks, fossils, antiques, and leather and rubber novelties. The middle of the street was a solid mass of hot, sweaty, horny gay men, shrieking, dishing, panting, laughing, all trying to squeeze by each other.

Applegate got to the door of the Blue Gardenia and managed to wedge himself inside. Throckmorton, as always, shone out in the crowd, and Applegate worked his way in Throckmorton's direction.

When he got a few feet from the bar, Applegate saw Matthew sitting next to Throckmorton. Suddenly Matthew's face twisted in rage as he pointed towards Applegate and shouted, "You!"

The bartender quickly ran out from behind the bar and rushed towards Applegate with a billy club raised menacingly in his hand. Matthew was mouthing, "I'm gonna break your arms!" (or maybe "You lousy motherfucker"; Applegate didn't read lips as well as he read meaning). Suddenly the bartender stepped past Applegate and grabbed the man behind Applegate, whom they had really been shouting at. Applegate turned and saw it was Pinkerton. The bartender dragged Pinkerton out of the bar.

While all this was going on, another conversation was taking place a few feet below.

"Pretty exciting, huh?"

Guildenstern looked up at the sea of gay faces. "So many gorgeous apartments! So little time!"

"Just imagine the draperies! The artwork!"

"The track lighting! The plush carpet!"

"Thousands of little nooks and crannies!"

"Closets full of clothes! Oceans of kitchen appliances!"

"Crumbs from cuisinarts!"

"Cashmere and silk!"

"Feathers and hats!"

Rosencrantz hopped onto the inner hem of Pinkerton's trousers. Guildenstern followed just as the bartender was dragging Pinkerton away. Rosencrantz said, "Something tells me to go home with this guy. Applegate doesn't need us anymore. But this guy's just crying out for us."

Guildenstern exclaimed, "The gypsy roaches!" and proceeded to do his impersonation of Judy Garland singing "Anywhere I hang my hat is home."

Rosencrantz looked very serious (difficult to discern in a cockroach, especially one as prone to irony as Rosencrantz) and said, "I think it's time we settled down." His facial exoskeleton seemed to glow as he looked longingly into Guildenstern's ocular antennae and said, in a shy, halting voice, "I want to spawn."

"Oh Rosie! Do you mean it? Little brown roaches of our very own?"

"Yes, I want to overrun the new apartment. Something tells me that this Pinkerton character needs a lot of education."

"How do you know his name is Pinkerton?"

"We're roaches. We're omniscient."

"I didn't know that."

"Trust me."

"So, who'll be the female?"

"We'll take turns. I'll lay the first thousand; then you can lay the next thousand."

"Oh, Rosie! We'll be so happy! I'll be a good father. I won't be like my old man–I won't eat any of our kids. At least, not while they're alive."

"What if you get hungry?"

"Oh... well..."

Rosencrantz glanced at him suspiciously. "I think I'd better mind the nursery. Have you ever witnessed the miracle of birth?"

"Not that often. Maybe a quarter of a million times."

Rosencrantz could see it in his mind. "The jellied mucous with thousands of tiny black specks suspended throughout!"

Guildenstern snuggled up against Rosencrantz. "Barely held together by the gossamer membrane…"

"Then a quiver, a ripple…"

"A hesitant throb…"

"A bold protrusion!"

Guildenstern lost control, "And then an apocalypse of cockroaches!"

"What rapture!"

"What a feast!"

Rosencrantz asked severely, "Excuse me?"

"For the eyes! I meant a feast for the eyes."

"I see…"

Applegate watched Pinkerton being thrown out the door and then turned to Matthew. He saw Matthew's face soften. He realized Matthew was looking at him. He felt total confusion. He glanced to his right, and there was Jacques Hardoné waving at him in a very provocative manner. Chardonnay was close by, speaking with Kevin. Then Throckmorton was at Applegate's shoulder gaily exclaiming, "So glad you could make it! We're over here!" Applegate went along with Throckmorton to the bar.

"Applegate, this is my friend Matthew. Matt, you remember Applegate, don't you? He's been coming around here for a few months."

Matthew was frightened and confused–the sight of Applegate awed him. Applegate looked different: more open, more real… more challenging. Matt looked down shyly to the floor and mumbled, "Hi."

Applegate said earnestly, "No, I know you. You're not the one. I'm sorry."

Matthew looked up at him. "Sorry? For what?"

In a fog, Applegate blurted out, "I didn't spray you with tear gas!"

"You're sorry you didn't spray me with tear gas?"

"No, I mean… You're not the one I thought you were."

"The one which?"

Applegate shook his head a moment and extended his hand. "Hi, I'm Jerry Applegate. I'm very pleased to meet you."

Matt clasped his hand. "Jelly Mapplethorpe? That name sounds familiar. Did you once send me a real weird singing telegram?"

Minutes after establishing a loving rapproachment with Alex, Kevin was protesting his innocence. "I have no idea! He must have slipped it in there when I wasn't looking. I don't even know any Pinkerton. Can't we just go home and make love?"

Alex shrieked, "That's all you ever think about! I swear you only have two emotions! Three if you count hunger! You think that making love solves all problems!"

Kevin muttered in exasperation, "Oh, eat me–"

Alex's face brightened. "Really? You want to fuck! That's different! I thought you wanted to screw!"

Alex wasn't being sarcastic. Kevin could tell from the glow in Alex's face that he was turned on and sincere. Kevin muttered, "I'm sorry; I guess I forgot to bring my relationship dictionary–"

"You big old gummy-bear!"

"The fight's over?"

Alex snuggled up to him and licked his ear. "As soon as we get home, I'll make some hollandaise sauce and you can dribble it over my–"

Kevin grabbed Alex's arm and rushed out the door. "Let's hurry! We haven't a moment to lose! *Carpe diem!*"

"The day isn't the only thing I want to seize!"

Raymond, the Vietnam vet (and former dog breeder) from Michigan, was once again "between homes" and trying to arrange for a place to live. In an obscure corner, Paris was saying to him, "We'll try it for a few weeks. You get room and board. If you need more money, you'll have to take a part-time job somewhere else. Are you sure you can cook?"

"Like Julia Child."

"I hope you like dogs."

Raymond felt sick but looked cheerful. "Dogs? I grew up with dogs. I raised dogs. My last place, I ate, slept and breathed dogs." He muttered to himself, "Dogs on the couch, dogs in my bed, dogs in my fucking face…"

"Good, 'cause I have five."

Raymond asked, "What kind?" Somehow he knew what the answer would be.

"Shar-Peis!"

"Shar-Peis?"

"Shar-Peis! Do you know what they look like?"

Raymond ignored a wave of nausea and said, "Yeah, I know what Shar-Peis look like. You have five of them?"

"Yeah. Some people think five Shar-Peis in a city apartment is ludicrous, but we get along fine."

"Ludicrous? Well, sure. My old roommate made a lot of money…"

Not far away, Chardonnay and Eric were having a rapturous reconciliation. "I hate us being mad at each other. I want to pay for the rug. I really do. I have my checkbook on me. I'll write you a check."

Eric said, "No, not one of your checks. You have to make a deposit first."

Chardonnay sparkled, "A deposit?"

"Sure, you have to put money in before you can write me a check."

Chardonnay was inspired. "Don't worry, I've got it covered." She handed Eric a check for sixty dollars.

"Are you sure there's enough in the account to cover it?"

Chardonnay smiled wisely. "There will be in a minute. I'm writing a check now that I'll deposit into my account, and this check will more than cover yours!"

"Chardonnay!"

East of the moon, about 2 light years south of Venus, in the midst of a minor constellation which provided an excellent view of tonight's fair, Dutchman looked at his cards. As he hesitantly played the king of spades, he asked Elyssia, "Has he kissed him yet?"

She took the king with her ten and glanced across the galaxy to the corner of Halsted and Melrose. "Not yet, Angel. Another 10 minutes or so." She played her ace of spades.

"What's trump?"

Elyssia laughed a silver, shimmering laugh. "Hearts. You should know. You named it. Would you like some more absinthe, Pumpkin?"

"Please." She picked up the crystal decanter and half-filled his glass with the emerald liquid.

Dutchman took the ace with his nine of hearts. Elyssia asked, "So, all this heartache and we don't even know if Damen is gay?"

"Not for sure. But I've heard a lot of rumors about him and Pythias. I'll find out tomorrow. We're playing tennis."

"He's awfully cute. If he turns out to be straight, tell him you have a friend."

As Dutchman played his ten of clubs, he asked, "Are you clumping trubs?"

She trumped it with her jack of hearts and sighed, "Oh lord…"

"She wanted to smack me for asking you what kind of beer you were drinking? What is she, some sort of fanatical prohibitionist?"

"No, she thought… it's kind of a long story. We thought you were Pinkerton and…"

As Applegate tried to untangle the chronology, Matthew was startled by Applegate's eyes. They were brown, and now, in the glow from the jukebox, they softened to a very special shade of russet.

A decade earlier, when Matthew had begun listening to opera, he had become fascinated by a particular aria. It was Mussetta's song in act two of *La Boheme*, the sweeping, vast waltz she sings about the raptures of desire. For months Matt had tried to learn the melody so that he could hum it to himself, but somehow it always escaped him. Matt had no training in music and would become confused by the delicate twists and turns the song makes. No matter how hard he tried, it was always just beyond his grasp.

Then one night, he had a dream in which the entire aria came to him in a single moment. Every note, every nuance, every crystalline shimmer was manifest. After that dream, the music was his own. He had never forgotten a single note.

Now, looking at Applegate, Matt had a similar experience. The russet-brown of Applegate's eyes brought back the afternoon, long past, when Matt and Roger had ditched their classes and gone to the forest preserves. Roger had brought along his guitar that day, and now, in a single moment, Matt heard every note Roger had played.

Every chord, every melody, every harmony of voice and instrument ran through Matt's mind in an instant. All the passion for life and love of the human race which Roger had played on the guitar that day infused itself into Matthew's soul. Matt knew it was a permanent part of him, that it would always be waiting for him whenever he needed it. It was almost as though Roger were playing it for him right now.

Jacques Hardoné walked up to Chardonnay. "You have wonderful hair, you know that? What's your name?"

"I'm Chardonnay."

Jacques was hypnotized by her hair. "May I run my fingers through it?"

"Of course!"

"Ohhhh, so soft, so pretty."

She gazed at him and asked, "Do you like my eyes?"

Jacques admired them. "They're perfect."

"And these earrings?"

"Lovely.

Chardonnay asked, "They go great with my skin color and hair, don't they?"

"You know what I love the most?"

"What?"

Jacques smiled, "Well, I couldn't help but notice in the mirror behind you… I couldn't help but notice how the lights in here produce an auburn sheen off my hair."

Chardonnay stiffened up. "*Your* hair?"

Jacques looked beyond her as he mused, "See how the sparkle seems to dance around my head, almost like a halo?"

Chardonnay stroked Jacques' hair. "My favorite is how this peasant blouse makes me look busty, like those women in old pirate movies."

Jacques said excitedly, "Or how about the way, if I stand just right, the mirrors reflect each other, producing an infinity of Jacques Hardonés…"

Chardonnay was not as entranced by Jacques as she had originally been. She asked, "Are you from around here?"

"I'm from California. I'm in Chicago to be in a gangster movie."

"You're an actor, aren't you?"

"Yeah." He thought to himself, "Gee, what tipped you off?"

"Do you know Robert DeNiro?"

"No, he's never been in any of my pictures."

"Do you think he'd be easy to work with?"

"I don't–"

Chardonnay interrupted, "I bet he demands a lot of perks."

"Well, some stars–"

"Do you think he has his dinner brought to the studio?"

Jacques began, "Probably, if–"

"Or maybe he has his own chef there to fix it for him?"

"It's possib–"

"Or maybe he has it delivered from his favorite restaurant."

"That could–"

"Or from several different restaurants, a different one every night. There are a lot of restaurants in Hollywood, aren't there?"

Jacques tried to edge into the conversation, "I don't work in Hollywood itsel–"

"How many?"

"How many what?"

Chardonnay looked at Jacques in exasperation. "How many restaurants are there in Hollywood?"

Jacques rubbed his chin and began, "Oh, I'd guess about–"

"Do you think Robert DeNiro eats light? A lot of salads and fish?"

"Most stars these days–"

"Or does he like steak?"

"Well, sure, I'm sure–"

Chardonnay interrupted him, "With french fries? Or baked potato?"

"Who? Robert DeNiro?"

Chardonnay laughed, "How about you?"

"Are you asking me if I like french fries?"

"No, do you like Robert DeNiro?"

"Sure, I'd like to fu–"

"Who's your favorite star?"

Jacques looked thoughtful as he responded, "I really admire Florence Henderson. I think her work in *The Brady Bunch* defined the role of contemporary woman."

Chardonnay asked, "Do you like this necklace?"

Jacques held out his hand. "Do you like this ring?"

Stalemate. Chardonnay suddenly exclaimed, "Wait a minute! I've seen you before!"

Jacques smiled and asked, with very convincing "aw shucks" modesty, "Which movie?"

"No, at Jerry Applegate's! I go to him for my migraines."

"Applegate? You go to Applegate, too? Yeah, I see him whenever I'm in town."

"For migraines?"

"I get 'em something fierce. Plus I like to smoke dope with him."

"Jerry Applegate? High?"

"Sure."

Chardonnay was excited at the image. "What's he like when he's stoned?"

Jacques smiled his Jacques Hardoné smile. "Oh, man, you ought to try it sometime. He gets so blitzed... so blitzed I can actually convince him he's flying. He's a riot."

"I'll bring some pot to my next session with him."

"If you do, tell him he's dreaming and you're not really there. Trust me, he'll believe you."

"So about your movie–who's your leading lady?"

"Lady? Well, there isn't exactly any–"

"What's the plot?"

Jacques loved talking about the new film. "The Roaring Twenties. I play Elliot Ness, and I'm always chasing after Al Capone. But not exactly like in *The Untouchables*. This is something new for me, a sort of cross-over movie that might go into the general market. We were hoping to film part of it at the Green Mill Lounge, but they weren't real keen on the idea."

"The jazz club up by Lawrence?"

"Yeah. It was Capone's favorite bar when he was alive."

"What's his favorite bar now?"

"Anyway, there's this great scene where I say, 'You like having that big dick up my ass, don't you, Scarface?'"

Even Dr. Bellman was here tonight. He was with Ogden, Dutchman's short, hawk-nosed curmudgeon friend, the one who had once railed to Applegate that the Blue Gardenia was a meat rack. Ogden put his arms around Bellman. "Hey, sugar britches, what say we go back to my place? I got a two-pound can of Crisco with your name on it."

Bellman laughed rapturously. "Jesus! Don't you ever stop to rest!?"

As the two men hugged, Bellman caught sight of Applegate. Bellman and Applegate smiled at each other. Bellman nodded. Applegate sighed as Bellman and Ogden walked out the door.

Matthew looked quizzically into Applegate's face. Finally Matt asked, "Do you want to go... for a cup of coffee somewhere?"

The intensity in Applegate's voice matched Matthew's. "Sure. How about my place?"

Matt nodded vigorously, "Sure. You have coffee?"

"Yeah I have… of course I have… uh, no, I don't have any coffee, but we can stop at the store and get a pound…"

"That's okay, I didn't really mean coffee…"

"Good, 'cause I just remembered, I don't own a coffee-maker…" Applegate's face brightened as he almost shouted, "But I do have some Spumoni ice cream!"

"Spumoni's not coffee-flavored. You're thinking of Jamoca."

"Right! That's what I meant! It is Jamoca!"

"I love Jamoca."

"But I finished it off last week… "

As they stood in front of the Blue Gardenia, the crescent moon above lolled on its back. Matthew asked, "Shall we walk to your place? Or do you want to cail a hab?"

Applegate was unaware of the consonant switch. He offered, "We could bake a tus."

"No, I'm not hungry."

They began to glide down Halsted Street. Matt whispered, "Let's just walk, okay? This is the most beautiful sky I've ever seen, and I want to savor it."

Applegate impulsively kissed him on the cheek. Matt could only respond, "Uhhhhhhhhhhhhhh… "

The End

Greek Youth Study I © 1986

Encircling I © 1994

Internationally-known photographer David Grinnell captures the male form in all its beauty and grace. From insightful character studies to stunning displays of form, Grinnell's work motivates and inspires. He captures not only the essence of maleness and masculinity, going beyond trendy physique candids, but the softness, vulnerability and empowerment of the body. His work has been featured in many books and magazines as well as displayed in major galleries across the country.

Grinnell expands the classic nude into depths seldom explored by other modern photographers.

Privation of the Mount © 1990

David Grinnell is pleased to offer limited-edition, signed and numbered museum prints. 11x14 prints $95.00 and 16x20 prints are $120.00. A catalog is also available of other current works (limited editions, T-shirts, etc.).

TITLE	QTY	PRICE
CATALOG ($2.00)		
TOTAL		

Please make payment (check, money order) and inquires to :
Grinnell Graphiques
2227 Essex St., Baltimore, MD 21231

Please send me the current catalog of available fine art photography by David Grinnell. I have enclosed payment of $2.00

NAME: _____

ADDRESS: _____

_____

CITY/STATE/ZIP: _____

SIGNATURE: _____

MUST BE 21 YEARS OF AGE IN THE USA, 18 YEARS OF AGE IN CANADA TO ORDER